YC

5-7-98

SR

BE MY GUEST

Elizabeth Cadell

Chivers Press   Thorndike Press
Bath, England • Thorndike, Maine USA

This Large Print edition is published by Chivers Press, England, and by Thorndike Press, USA.

Published in 1998 in the U.K. by arrangement with Severn House Publishers Ltd.

Published in 1998 in the U.S. by arrangement with Brandt & Brandt Literary Agency, Inc.

U.K. Hardcover ISBN 0–7540–3111–X (Chivers Large Print)
U.S. Softcover   ISBN 0–7862–1107–5 (General Series Edition)

The text of this Large Print edition is unabridged.
Other aspects of the book may vary from the original edition.

Set in 16 pt. New Times Roman.

Printed in Great Britain on acid-free paper.

British Library Cataloguing in Publication Data available

Library of Congress Cataloging-in-Publication Data

Cadell, Elizabeth.
  Be my guest / by Elizabeth Cadell.
    p.   cm.
  ISBN 0–7862–1107–5 (large print : sc : alk. paper)
  1. Large type books.   I. Title.
[PR6005.A225B4   1998]
823'.914—dc21   97–12433

CHAPTER ONE

It was a good year for strawberries. It was a good year, in fact, for all the fruit and flowers and vegetables in Mr. Channing's beloved garden. The lawns, upper and lower, the rose beds, the borders were looking better than he ever remembered seeing them; in the kitchen garden beyond the neatly scalloped hedge, peas, gooseberries and currants, beans, asparagus, lettuces and potatoes and cucumbers were all thriving. His grapes were hanging in promising green bunches. In the orchard, his fruit trees were laden and pest-free. Viewing the well-ordered, productive scene, Mr. Channing reflected that Nature, this year, had been kind; it had been a mild spring and there had been no late frosts.

But while giving Nature her due, he could not help feeling that a good deal of the credit must go to himself. What he saw around him was certainly Nature's bounty, but it was also his own hard work, his own unremitting care and devotion and vigilance. Without his labour, Nature, in however benevolent a mood, could not have painted this picture of perfection. He would not have voiced this conviction in the presence of others, but when he came out each morning before breakfast to make a tour of his domain, he allowed himself

1

a measure of praise.

His daily inspection over, it was his habit to go straight into breakfast, the meal he enjoyed more than any other—but today, when at last he turned and walked towards the house, his footsteps lagged. They'd still be crying, he reflected gloomily. His wife had cried half the night and he supposed that his daughter, in her own room, had cried all night. Breakfast, usually so pleasant, so peaceful an interlude, was today going to be in every sense a washout.

He turned and let his eyes wander round the quiet countryside that surrounded his property. The house was in one of the most rural districts of Hampshire; on all sides nothing was to be seen but well-tended fields and, in the distance, a farmhouse or two. He had bought the house on his marriage and had brought his wife here, turning a deaf ear to the gloomy prognostications of friends. It was the end of nowhere, they had pointed out; miles from a station, nowhere near a bus route, difficult to get to and even more difficult to get out of. It was not within easy reach of London, there wasn't a sign of a shop and the nearest hamlet was three miles away; was he going to immure his wife and, later, his children in this out-of-the-way spot?

He was, and did. The house was solid, the gardens extensive; the remote situation kept the price down and gave him something that he sought in all his financial dealings: value for money. He had no need, since his solicitor's office was situated in a Hampshire town, to worry about getting to London. His wife could get to the shops, he to the station in a car; for the rest, there would be space, and peace. Peace and quiet, and a garden to work in when he retired—could a man ask more? Mr. Channing thought not. He had retired at the unusually early age of fifty, and for the sixteen years that had passed since then, could claim to have worked a full day, every day, for the most part unassisted, on his twelve beloved acres—eight of them paddock. His wife had not complained of the distance from London or the shops; his children had kept their ponies in the paddock and had run free in those parts of the garden set aside for recreation. He himself had lived a quiet, withdrawn, busy life, leaving social distractions to those who enjoyed them.

He turned reluctantly towards the house once more and walked towards it, pausing to inspect moodily his wife's patch of garden—a row of herbs whose names he found confusing and whose use he had prohibited in dishes cooked for his consumption; he wanted good, plain English fare and you could keep your basil and your thyme and all the rest of them. But it amused Madeleine to grow them, and for the next few weeks, she'd need all the amusement she could find.

Anger—slow, unaccustomed—rose in him and he fought it down. Damn them. Damn

3

them for bringing into this peaceful spot, into his wife's and his own peaceful lives, this trouble and turbulence. Belted earl be ... be damned. His own family and his wife's family were of as good stock as anything you could find between the covers of Debrett: solid, sober Englishmen and women doing their duty and going quietly about their business and upholding traditions of honesty and dignity. Blast all earls.

He kicked aside a pebble and gazed at his house. Small by their standards, no doubt, but in his view infinitely more comfortable. While they'd all been hanging on to their ancient glories, he'd been adapting his household to changed conditions, and he wouldn't change this place for any number of castles. Nor would his wife, Madeleine.

His daughter...

Well, he'd better go inside and tell her to stop crying.

He walked round to a door at the side of the house and entered the small, stone-floored hall that was known as the garden room. Here he kept his gardening boots and some of his smaller gardening tools; on the round, marble-topped table he always placed the day's picking of fruit and vegetables. In the huge jar in the corner, his wife kept flowers until she was ready to arrange them in vases. Neatness, order; the house, from top to bottom, shining, glowing, kept immaculate by his wife with the

4

help of a neighbouring farmer's daughter, who liked the job because heavy labour had been reduced to a minimum. Forethought; planning. He'd rather be here, unlacing his boots and going in to a well-cooked breakfast, than wandering round a mouldering ancestral castle wondering if the time had come to let the public in at three shillings a head.

He put on his indoor shoes and walked into the dining-room. The door at the far end opened into the kitchen, and he could see his wife standing before the gleaming white stove. The dining-table was spread with a pale yellow cloth; coffee bubbled in an electric percolator, a fireproof jug containing hot milk stood over a low flame.

This was the moment he most looked forward to, when his wife, trim and smiling, brought in toast and porridge and set it before him, when she sat down and poured out his coffee, when he ate his porridge and tried to guess what was coming next: eggs and bacon, kidneys and tomatoes, a couple of kippers or a nice bit of haddock. He never asked and she never told him. She knew what he liked and how he liked it, and she gave it to him. Was the earl, he wondered, sitting down to a meal like this in a setting like this?

He stole a glance at his wife as she put his plate of porridge before him. She was weeping silently, wiping away tears.

'I thought you said'—he spoke gruffly—

'that you weren't going to let it worry you.'

'I was thinking of Christine.'

'She'll get over it. You wait and see.'

'She won't, Bruce. I keep telling you that this time, it's serious.'

'Nonsense. How many young men has she—'

'She's in love; deeply in love.'

They had been repeating this conversation almost without variation since yesterday afternoon, when their youngest daughter, Christine, had returned unheralded from what they had imagined to be a full and useful and happy life in London. She had not, it was true, been home since Christmas, but her letters, her chats on the telephone, had seemed as cheerful as usual. Nothing had prepared them for yesterday's stormy, red-eyed reappearance.

They sat in silence for a time. Mr. Channing wondered what he ought to do about the matter, and as usual decided to wait for his wife to tell him. It was an arrangement that had worked very well for almost thirty years.

She had been twenty when he married her. He had been thirty-seven—a large, lumbering, red-haired man, handsome in a heavy way, slow of speech, shy and miserable in company, anxious to efface himself in his work and, later, in his garden. His affection for his wife still held a large proportion of gratitude: she had loved him, married him, given him a handsome son and three distractingly pretty daughters, had

6

run his house efficiently and shielded him from all avoidable social contacts. She had dealt with Headmasters and mistresses and later had entertained tirelessly the unending succession of young men and women who came crowding the house. She had married off two of their daughters to pleasant young businessmen and had steered their son into a union with a charming young woman. Most of this Mr. Channing had watched from behind the shelter of his bushes and hedges. He had sought no authority, and had therefore further reason to be grateful to a wife who had never allowed him to lose his place as head of the family, who had transmitted to all four children the protective affection she felt for him and had strangled at birth any criticism of his escapist tendencies or of his rather ponderous speech and thought.

A sense of resentment swept over him. The others—Barbara and Antoinette and, only three weeks ago, Neville—had all managed to get themselves married without fuss. There had been none of this crying and confusion, none of this hold-up. Plain misters had done very well for the other two girls; why should this fellow have been allowed to come along and make so much trouble, not only for Christine but for them all?

He scraped his plate and put down his spoon angrily. Peace; that was all he asked. How could a man be at peace when his wife and sole remaining daughter were drowning themselves in tears?

'Where is she?' he asked.

'In her room. When she comes downstairs, I think you ought to say something to her. She's so unhappy, Bruce.'

'I talked to her yesterday,' he said, 'and what good did it do? None. She didn't even listen.'

The matter, he felt, ought to be allowed to simmer for a time. You couldn't really say much to a girl who wept in a way you hadn't seen her weep since her gas balloon went up and failed to come down again. It upset him. He would have been angry to be accused of having a favourite among his children, but there was no doubt that this youngest, twenty-two-year-old daughter did something to him that Barbara and Antoinette and even his son, Neville, had failed to do. Yesterday had shaken him badly.

He uncovered the dish that his wife had set before him. Kidneys and bacon. The bacon sizzling, the kidneys in rich brown gravy. Why couldn't a man be allowed to enjoy his breakfast?

'You didn't really talk to her,' his wife said. 'All you did was swear.'

He could not deny it. Never quick to grasp the heart of any matter, it had taken him some time to reach the source of his daughter's unhappiness. Having at last managed to take in the astounding fact that an interfering old

8

earl in a crumbling castle somewhere up in Northumberland didn't consider Christine good enough for his grandson, he had, to his own astonishment, called him some names he had been hardly aware that he knew.

'Talking,' he pointed out, 'won't have any effect on her in the state she's in now.'

Even, he added to himself, if he could find anything to say. The best thing he could do was get himself out of the way until the thing could be discussed on a dry basis. He searched for a means of escape and fortunately found one.

'I've got to go to the station to pick up those crates,' he said.

Mrs. Channing checked herself on the point of reminding him that the crates containing his son's wedding presents could very well wait at the station for another day or two; Neville and his bride were on their way to Budapest and would not be needing them for the next two years. Instead, she brought hot toast and placed it at his elbow and pushed the marmalade nearer. He finished his breakfast, kissed his wife, walked through the kitchen into the garage and drove away in the family car: a shabby but serviceable station-wagon. As the sound of his departure died away, the dining-room door opened and a face—framed in uncombed hair of the same shade of red that Mr. Channing's had once been—appeared round it.

'Has he gone?' Christine enquired.

'Yes. Come in.'

Christine came in, pulled out a chair, sat down and poured herself out some coffee.

'No—just coffee,' she said, checking her mother's movement towards the kitchen. 'I couldn't eat; it would choke me.'

Mrs. Channing studied her and felt very much relieved; her daughter's face was pale and tear-stained, but she had recovered her look of calm good sense and even something of her humour.

'You look as though you'd been howling all night,' she told her mother.

'Not all night. From ten to twelve.'

'That must have cheered Father. Did he have any new swear words to offer this morning?'

'No. He said he had to go and collect Neville's crates, and I didn't stop him.'

'I suppose he's still saying I'll get over it?'

'One gets over most things. You may think your father slow, but he's sound. You can't blame him for being bewildered. This thing must have been going on for the past six months, but you told us nothing at all about it. Did you say anything to Barbara and Antoinette?'

'I took James to see them.'

'Why didn't you bring him to see us?'

'I'd brought so many men home. I thought you'd think he was just another of them—and he wasn't.'

'Your father asked me about him last night. I couldn't tell him anything because I didn't know anything—not even when or where you and James met one another. I thought it was about December, but he wasn't one of the people you brought home for Christmas.'

'I hadn't met him then. If you remember, I went back to London two days after Christmas.'

'Yes. There was a dance or something.'

'That was the one. I went with a party—six of us. James was there with some other people. We just looked at one another and that was that. I went home after the dance feeling most peculiar, and he said he did too. He tried to find out who I was, but he made the mistake of asking Charles Granger—and Charles, being after me himself, told him I was a Miss Henrietta Cook who lived with a widowed mother near Battersea Park. He gave James the telephone number, which turned out to be the Battersea Dogs' Home. So that didn't get James very far.'

'Did you know, that first night, who he was?'

'No. I made the same mistake as James—I went to Charles for information. He told me that James was a man called Oscar Blake, who was waiting for a divorce from his wife and was going to marry the girl in blue he was dancing with. And you can say what you like, but if it had been meant to be just an ordinary affair, we'd have stuck there and nothing more would have happened. But James, thinking hard after the Dogs' Home check, remembered that I'd spoken to old Mrs. Spender at the dance. He knew her by sight and remembered that her husband had something to do with cars. In a big way, of course. So he started in the showrooms and made his way up slowly until he reached Mr. Spender's secretary. He took her into his confidence and made her promise to wring some information out of Mrs. Spender next time she dropped into the office. So the secretary got Mrs. Spender talking about the dance—James had practically written the script for her—and found out that the girl in pale floating green—James's description of my dress—was called Channing. He worked down the Channings in the phone book and at last came to Aunt Elinor, who thanked him for having found her niece's bracelet and told him where to return it. Is that love,' demanded Christine, 'or isn't it?'

'Next?'

'He came to the flat. I was alone. He told me how he'd found me, but naturally, I didn't say anything about having asked Charles myself. When he told me his name, we discovered that he could have saved himself a lot of trouble, because I was at school with a distant cousin of his called Willa. Willa and her husband were at the dance, but he hadn't thought of asking her.'

Mrs. Channing said nothing, being unwilling to check the flow of reminiscence, but she thought it would be as well, when relaying the facts to her husband, to suppress the Willa bit; when he began to look about him in order to apportion blame, he would without doubt begin by reminding her that he had always considered her choice of school for their daughters expensive and unsuitable and certain to instil in them extravagant ways which he would not have the means to indulge.

'Go on,' she urged Christine.

'Well, there's nothing more to say. We were in love. It was as different as anything I ever felt before as ... as ... well, it was quite different. We didn't want to go about, for one thing. We used to wander round the parks, if you ever heard anything crazier. We used to walk, and talk, eat in snack bars and then walk and talk again. It was a bad winter, people said, but I wouldn't know. I never knew bare trees could be so beautiful. We used to try to be out early on snowy mornings, so's to be the first to make footprints. The men I'd known before were around somewhere, but they must have seen they were wasting their time. I dimly remember handing them their hats—but only dimly. There was only James. He had to be at this college during the week, but he used to drive up to town most evenings and we'd meet outside my office. And as far as I could see, there was nothing to do but wait until we came out of our coma, tell our respective families that we were going to get married—and get married. Last week, we decided the time had come, so James went up to Northumberland to talk to his grandfather, and then we were coming down here together.'

'Did you know that James's grandfather was likely to make trouble?'

'How could I know? It was only lately that I learned that James had a grandfather; I'd assumed he had parents like everybody else. But they've been dead for years, and he was brought up by his grandfather at this castle up in Northumberland. James had an idea there might be a hitch, but he didn't say anything to me before going north. He knew there'd be a row, because as long as he can remember, there's always been the same trouble: money. Lack of. The castle sucks up money as vampires suck blood, and there was the Government and taxes and death duties and I can't remember what else. The point is that there's no money and nothing but land left to sell, but James's grandfather hadn't worried too much about the future because on the one side there was James and a future earldom, and on the other side was this Katherine Staples and her three millions.'

There was a pause. Mrs. Channing grew pale.

'You didn't,' she said, keeping her voice expressionless, 'say anything yesterday about Katherine Staples. Who is she?'

'James's cousin. She's not, from James's

point of view, of any importance whatever. She's his second cousin and loaded, and James's grandfather decided long ago that she and James would marry and that would solve everything.'

'I see. And when James went home and—'

'He knew the old man was going to take it hard, but he had no idea how hard. When he broke the news, there was a row that rocked the battlements. James said it was fantastic—just like olden times: a ranting old man screeching at his rebellious heir because he wasn't going to bring an heiress home. Father got the idea yesterday that I wasn't considered up to social scratch—but I am. Family doesn't enter into this. It's just money, money, money.'

'And so?'

'And so James said he intended to marry me. And so his grandfather said that if he didn't say good-bye to me and marry the three millions, he could say good-bye to the rest, such as it is, of his inheritance. And so—'

'How much,' interrupted Mrs. Channing, 'is it?'

'It's what's left of what was once a pretty big spread of country. The family started off as Border chiefs; that's to say, they used to take off every now and then over the Border into Scotland, picking up what they could, including some just-widowed beautiful women. They robbed, and grew rich. The earldom came later, and brought in an estate or two which the second earl promptly gambled away. What with that and the dwindling opportunities for pillage and plunder, things have been going from bad to worse for the past few hundred years, and the family's had to slice considerable slices off their land. Now they're down to a village or two, some farms and the castle precincts, and if James marries me, his grandfather's going to start selling off the last few thousand acres. And that's the core of the trouble. James loves every square yard of the land, and every tree and stone on it. He doesn't agree that he won't be able to hang on to what's left; he came down to spend a year at an Agricultural College to learn how to make some of his ideas work. He's sure he can keep going—but he came back from the interview with his grandfather and told me that if he hadn't arranged this form of compromise, the old man would have put the sale in hand then and there. So they made their terms.'

'James to see nothing of you for three months?'

'Yes. He's to go home and not see me or write to me. When he told me, I was so angry that I . . .'

'You came home.'

'Yes. It seemed to me treacherous of him to have agreed to keep away from me when he knew that for the whole of the three months, his ghastly grandfather would have a last try at marrying him off to Katherine Staples and her money. He went so far as to tell James he'd compromised her.'

'And had he?'

'How could he? The word's obsolete. James asked her to a Commem. Ball when he was up at Oxford, and he once escorted her to Ascot, and he was photographed with her at the Dublin Horse Show. I dare say in his grandfather's day that would have got her really talked about.'

'Does James like her?'

'He says he's got nothing against her; she's a nice girl, and very bright by the sound of it, but he's not interested in her matrimonially, nor she in him. That isn't the trouble. The trouble is that James is in love with his land and he thinks that three months' privation isn't too much to endure for the sake of it. I disagreed, and told him so—very strongly. Then I came home.'

Her mother studied her.

'And now?'

Christine poured out the rest of the coffee and drank it.

'Crying all night,' she said, 'washes the dust off the brain. I came downstairs at five o'clock this morning and rang James up and told him to come down here today. He's coming to lunch. He said yesterday—before I told him I was leaving him for ever—that he owed it to you and to Father to come down and explain the position. So he's coming.'

'But what's he coming *for*?'

'Mummy, I've just *said*. He's coming to talk over the position with you and with Father.'

'Yes, I heard that. But what *is* the position?'

'I explained it all in detail. James has agreed to wait for three months, and during that time—'

'James agreed, yes. But last night you said that—'

'Last night was last night. I was angry, and I wasn't thinking straight. I *told* you—I rang James up early this morning and said that perhaps he did owe it to his grandfather to wait a little while. It was a terrible blow to the old man, and James is all he's got, and I needn't have shouted at him and rushed down here.'

'You're going to wait?'

'Yes.'

'Without seeing James or writing to him?'

'Yes. If it's taken you so long to get the thing clear, how on earth am I ever going to hammer it into Father's thick skull?'

'Don't talk like that about your father,' Mrs. Channing said from years of habit. 'I'll tell him you've changed your mind about waiting.'

'How d'you know he won't look at this from that old man's point of view? You know what Father is about money.'

'Your father isn't mean, Christine. I wish you wouldn't all keep—'

'Will you make him talk to James? I don't mean talk to him, of course; all he'll do is what he did with Nigel and Max when Barbara and

18

Antoinette got engaged: he'll stand there, clear his throat, mumble, say Well-well-I-think-that-covers-everything, and go back to his garden. It isn't much, but at least James will be able to go back and tell his grandfather that my parents were behind me.'

Mrs. Channing thought that the earl had displayed singularly little interest in Christine or her parents, but she did not say so. Not saying so was an art which she had perfected to the highest degree. Not saying so had deprived her on many occasions of some fugitive satisfaction, but had in the long run won the gratitude and devotion of her family.

'Your father will talk to him,' she said, 'but there really isn't much he can say.'

'He can say that I'm not doing this for that money-grubbing old madman, but for James. He can ... Oh well, what's the use?'

Her calm, factual manner deserted her. She pushed away her cup, put her head down on the table and gave way to a flood of tears. Her mother went to her and, turning her chair round, transferred the wet face to her shoulder.

'There, there; don't cry, Christine darling,' she crooned. 'It'll be all right. Everything will be all right.'

She was glad to hear the note of confidence in her voice; she would have liked to feel as sanguine as she sounded. But the thought of the next three months weighed heavily on her, and she was further handicapped by her lack of knowledge of the man for whom her daughter was weeping. It was a pity Christine had not brought him home; she might have guessed what was to come, and she might have been able to give him more than the rather abstracted attention and politeness she accorded to her children's guests. She could have taken stock, tried to weigh him up. Now it was too late. She would have to make what she could of him when he came today, and assess as best she could her daughter's chances of happiness.

And before that, she remembered, she would have to reorganize the menu for lunch, send Christine in the car, when it returned, for two chickens, press the Madeira table mats, polish the sherry glasses, change the drawing-room flowers, put on a dress that would look nice without looking specially put on, and induce her husband to present a polite front to the man who had made his favourite daughter miserable.

She had, she discovered presently, to do more than that. Her husband returned from his errand with a red, angry face and no crates. Going out to the station-wagon, Mrs. Channing saw that it was empty and thought she could guess the reason for Mr. Channing's annoyance.

'They went to the junction instead, I suppose?' she said.

'What did?' Mr. Channing demanded in a

20

fierce voice.

'The crates.'

'The what?'

'The crates. Neville's crates. The crates they had the wedding presents packed into.'

'Oh, those. I didn't go to the station.'

He marched into the house and Mrs. Channing, mystified, followed him. To her surprise, he led her to the drawing-room and closed the door carefully behind him.

'Where did you go?' she enquired.

'I went to the library, that's where I went. The public library.'

'What on earth for?'

Her surprise was natural. Her husband was not a reader. He subscribed to *Country Life* and took in *The Times*, and found these sufficient for his literary needs. On the rare occasions on which he was confined to bed, he read Sherlock Holmes, the Bible and W. W. Jacobs. Libraries had never interested him.

'I went,' he said, in answer to his wife's query, 'to look up that chap's pedigree.'

'To ...?'

'On my way to get those crates, I began to think, and I said to myself: What do we know about this earl? Nothing. The only way to find out was to look him up. So I looked him up. If I ever had any illusions about how most of those chaps came by their titles, I've got none now. Do you know what this fellow—'

'The family dates from—'

21

'I don't care when it dates from. They were originally Border chiefs and they did more burning and looting than all the other Border chiefs put together. What I looked up was when and how they came by the title, the earldom—and I did find out. Do you want to know?'

'Of course I want to know.'

'Then I'll tell you. One of the women of the family was lady-in-waiting at the court of I forget which King in sixteen something or other. She was . . . well, she was no better than she should be. She and the King . . . well, we needn't go too deeply into it. Their family motto is—'

' "We serve the King?" '

'Eh?'

'Or: "Everything comes to her who waits?" '

'Don't try to change the subject. Do you realize that that madman up there in Northumberland, who thinks Christine isn't good enough for his grandson, springs from a . . . a . . .'

'Yes, dear. But it was a long time ago.'

'I don't care when it was. She went to bed with the King, and—'

'—and the King belted the issue. That's all over, Bruce—but James is coming down today. Christine rang him up and he's coming to lunch, and after lunch he's going away for three months and they're not going to see one another or write to one another and you've got

22

to—'

'Do you mean to tell me that—'

'The earl has nothing against Christine, Bruce. This is purely money. They're impoverished, they're down to their last resources and the fact that his grandson had fallen in love with a girl who had no money was a great shock to the old man.'

'If they ever mention family to me,' breathed Mr. Channing fiercely, 'I'll be able to tell them a thing or two.'

'Yes, dear. But nobody's going to mention family.'

'Your family and my family are—'

'Yes, of course; everybody knows that, dear.'

'And no wantons in them, either,'

'No, of course not. All Christine wants you to do is have a little talk with James and—'

'Just let him drag in family, that's all. A waiting-maid who—'

'I'll tell Christine the story and she can use it whenever James gets above himself. You ought to change your shirt, Bruce; he'll be here soon.'

'What's the matter with my shirt?'

'James can't help what one of the women of his family did in the seventeenth century, and refusing to change your shirt won't—'

'*Now* you come to it,' said Mr. Channing.

'Come to what?'

'To what I was trying to say. To what I was trying to tell you. Title or no title, that's one thing we haven't got in *our* family.'

'What is?'

'Dirty linen,' said Mr. Channing.

CHAPTER TWO

Mr. Channing did not share his wife's regret at not having been able to form an opinion of the young man with whom Christine had fallen in love, for his children's friends had lately seemed to him indistinguishable one from another. He noted only that the girls had wild-looking hair, stark, unfeminine clothes and confident voices; the young men had fast cars, casual clothes and easy manners. He saw them only at meals, and then saw only those to right and left of him. He tried, and they tried, to find a common topic; he failed and they failed, the meal came to an end and they parted with mutual relief. Who they were he never knew; why they were there he knew well enough: the men wanted his pretty daughters and the girls were after his handsome son. The days of the chase were almost over; three out of the four races had been run and his wife had satisfied herself, and him, that Barbara was very happy with Nigel and that Max and Antoinette were perfectly suited. As Neville had only married three weeks ago, it was not possible to say more than that he had got hold of a nice, steady,

24

sensible girl.

Three married, one to go. Mr. Channing, while rejecting any suggestion that one of his children meant more to him than the others, had nevertheless to admit that he would be sorry to see Christine go; she would take with her the last of the youthful brightness and gaiety that had filled the house. He had prepared himself for a parting, had braced himself to meet it; he had told himself that he must put nothing in her way. His present anger sprang largely from the shock of discovering that somebody else had put something in her way.

The earl, he decided after thinking the matter over, was simply off his head. Everybody knew that these old families suffered from inbreeding and were far from sound; you only had to look at them. They were called, for want of a ruder word, eccentric. Here was a man who, without so much as a look at the girl his grandson wanted to marry, had brushed her aside. Burning under this high-handed treatment, Mr. Channing paused to wonder how he would have felt if the earl, after a look at Christine, had brushed her aside; he decided that it was better not to pursue this thought.

His anger, which seldom found vent in words, smouldered within him during the morning as he clipped and weeded and hoed. With anger was mingled apprehension, for he realized that this was one of the rare occasions on which he would be called upon by his wife to take an active part. He had been obliged to interview the two young men whom Barbara and Antoinette had at last fixed upon to marry, but nothing had been required of him but a few words to acknowledge what was already a fact. His future sons-in-law had done all the talking, he had mumbled a sentence or two and that was all. The present situation, however, called for something more. With a sinking heart he realized that he would be expected to speak up on behalf of his daughter. He could not remain silent and permit an autocratic earl to put her on a shelf for three months while he sought something better for his grandson.

It was, he decided at last, no use rehearsing speeches. He would say whatever came into his head, if anything came. He would say what he had to say, and if his feelings were any guide, he would say it strongly enough.

James arrived at midday. Mr. Channing, from a concealed look-out behind the tomato house, saw with some surprise that his car was not, after all, one of the fast sports models that had to be driven from a recumbent position; it was a modest black five-seater not unlike the Vicar's. Peering more closely, he saw a tall form emerging from the car and enfolding Christine in a close and apparently unending embrace. When at last the visitor raised his head, he saw a plain but strong face, firm lips and a reassuring look of common sense. So far, so good—but appearances were often deceptive; he would wait and see what the fellow had to say for himself. He would not, unfortunately, have to wait long; he would soon have to go out there and show himself.

Misery flooded him. All his life shy to an almost pathological degree, he regarded talk as the bane of the modern world. There had always been talk, but in the old days nobody had been obliged to listen; all the talk was reported in the morning newspapers, to be read at breakfast or in the train on the way to the office. But nowadays most of the news in the papers was stale; it had been talked over on television the evening before, turned inside out, discussed, worried, analysed by experts, illuminated by maps and figures and statistics, switched to the trouble spot and brought back again for a summing up. If you listened, mused Mr. Channing resentfully, you went to bed with your ears buzzing and your mind in a turmoil. If you didn't listen, if you didn't follow what was going on not only in your own country but in the remotest parts of the world, you were written off as an escapist.

Escape, in fact, was what Mr. Channing had sought all his life and what he had achieved, in a great measure, since his marriage. His wife had protected him from all but their oldest, closest and quietest friends; she had shielded him from droppers-in—in his view thieves who stole from others time that could be used in a hundred better ways. She had made it possible for him to avoid parties, especially cocktail parties, which he regarded as the lunatic fringe of entertainment. But today she was not going to shield or protect him; escape was impossible.

Mrs. Channing, walking with James and Christine across the lawn, paused to give her husband time to come out of hiding and assume a pose of dignity near one of the flower beds. She knew with what dread he was anticipating the meeting, and wondered fleetingly why she had not relieved him of the burden. This, the first problem of any magnitude that had presented itself in the affairs of his children, had created a situation requiring some finesse and even perhaps some subtlety, and he possessed little of either.

She caught sight of him in the kitchen garden, and some part of her noted with pride his great height and breadth, his noble head with the rust-grey hair, his huge, strong hands, his fierce-looking blue eyes. The powerful frame was used for nothing more strenuous than pulling up roots or building trellises; the noble head didn't have much inside it and the fierce expression, she knew, concealed timidity and a distaste for the task ahead of him—but she loved him and had never wished him other than he was. She would have liked to help him now, but it was his job and he had to do it.

The four met and exchanged greetings and

stood together for a time. They talked of the spell of sunny weather, the probability that it would mean rain in July and August, the tennis and cricket prospects and the difficulties that attended week-end travel on the roads. Then Mrs. Channing remembered that there was something indoors that required her attention, and drew Christine away. The two men watched their departure with varying degrees of regret.

Left alone with the visitor, Mr. Channing tried to think of something to say, but there seemed no satisfactory way of introducing the subject of ladies-in-waiting. James, waiting politely for him to lead off, told himself with an unexpected uprush of liking and compassion that this mouse in superman guise would be no match for his fiery old grandfather, and resolved that when the two met, he would see to it that the earl did not have it all his own way.

'Ah,' said Mr. Channing suddenly.

'Sir?'

Nothing more was heard for a few moments, and then Mr. Channing brought out a sentence or two.

'I'm not good at talking; never was. But I don't like this business. I don't like it at all.'

'If you mean this delay,' James said quietly, 'I'm with you, sir. But my grandfather's old, and fond of his own way, and he settled in his own mind, many years ago, that I'd have to

29

bring some money into the family. I don't agree with him. That is, I don't agree with his idea that without money, we'll have to sell off most of the land that's left. I think that with patience, and a good deal of reorganization, I can get things on to a sounder footing. Nothing practical has ever been done to stop the rot; all we've done is hang on and hope for the best. I'm trying to make my grandfather see that we can't live as we once did, but even so we can live. We can stop pouring money out on the castle, for one thing; it was designed as a fortress and not as a comfortable home. My grandfather will probably spend the next three months trying to head me off in the direction of an heiress. I shall spend them trying to persuade him that we can avoid parting with any more land.'

An old name, Mr. Channing heard himself saying, to his own astonishment, brought its responsibilities.

'It depends,' James said, 'on what you want to hang on to. If we'd filled the castle with treasures the nation couldn't afford to lose, if we'd produced any soldiers or sailors or statesmen of note, I might feel more of this sense of responsibility you talk about. As it is, I feel we've been lucky for a long time and if our luck's running out, we haven't too much to complain of. That's my own view; it isn't my grandfather's.'

'It mightn't be your son's, either.'

'It's my son I'm thinking of. It's my son, or my sons, I'm planning for. The castle can go, but not the land. I want to keep the land. It means ... well, it means a lot to me. A place can ... can get into your blood. I can't explain it very well, but there are trees, and a stretch of river, and woods and a bit of moorland and hills and ... Well, that's what I'd like to keep. The rest can go.'

Mr. Channing said nothing, but James became aware that the silence had nothing of awkwardness in it. Mr. Channing owned no woods, no stretch of river or bit of moorland— but he understood, to the depths of his being, the sentiments just expressed by the young man standing beside him.

He studied the blunt, honest face and measured the strong figure—as tall as his own, though less broad and heavy. Something stirred within him—an unformed, vague hope, a faint revival of dreams that had died. Here was someone who was speaking, at last, his own language. Here, beside him, was a man who felt as he felt but who was able to give voice to his feelings. Here was a young man who spoke as he would have liked his son to speak—failing his son, his sons-in-law. But his son's interests had been in sport and in travel and in the hope—now realized—of getting into the Foreign Office. His sons-in-law, good enough as husbands, had what he termed city minds. But here, at last, was a man whose feet

31

were not only on the ground, but deep in the soil, as were his own. This man would understand when he spoke of things near his heart like pests and sprays and fertilizers. This man thought as he thought: of the beauties and the productivity of the land he owned. This man was, like himself, dedicated to the service of the soil.

'It would be a pity,' he said at last, 'to let the place break up.'

'That's why my grandfather and I came to this agreement about waiting three months. Waiting won't change anything for me, but it'll give him time to turn things over in his mind. I know it's hard on Christine, and I'm sorry that she and I . . .'

He paused, this aspect of the situation striking him anew and robbing him of his fluency. Mr. Channing, looking at his moody expression, would have liked to tell him that he, Christine's father, no longer had any fears for her future, but the words would not come.

'We've time before lunch,' he said instead, 'to take a look round the garden, if you'd like to?'

'Let's go,' said James.

*   *   *

In the drawing-room, Christine stood staring anxiously out of the window.

'What's keeping them?' she asked her

mother. 'Shall I go and see?'

'No. Leave them.'

'But I just told you—they'll be standing out there waiting for Father to begin.'

'He won't have to begin; he'll just have to listen to what James says.'

'But good Heavens! James has had time, by now, to recite his entire family history from twelve hundred onwards. Why don't they come in? Do you think … They couldn't be quarrelling, could they?'

'No. Hasn't it occurred to you that they're very much alike?'

'*Alike?*'

'In spirit. They're both land-lovers.'

Christine sat on the window-seat to consider this.

'Does that mean,' she asked at last, 'that I'll have to stick all my life in one place, as you've done?'

'It wasn't all my life. I did quite a lot of travelling before I married.'

'Well, all I've seen is a bit of France and Spain. Won't I ever get James off his land?'

'You might. He'll probably take you around—but his heart won't be in it. He'll be glad, and you'll be glad because he's glad, to get back home.'

'And that,' Christine said slowly, 'is the devilish part of marriage.'

'Yes,' her mother agreed tranquilly. 'It is.'

'Never'—Christine groped her way into the

future—'never again to enjoy anything, unless he's there.'

'That's about it.'

'But all this theory about getting away from one another, taking separate holidays, keeping the relationship fresh?'

'As you said: theory. If the marriage is sound, it stays fresh. If you love your husband, as I think you're doomed to do all your life, just as Barbara and Antoinette are doomed—'

'Couldn't we just say destined?'

'If you like. You'll all be faithful-unto-death wives because you're like me. It isn't a thing you can explain on moral or even on physical grounds; it's just being married. You simply want to be where your husband is, that's all. You can read all those travel folders about Venice, and imagine yourself gliding along in a gondola, or you can read about Florence and imagine yourself gazing with a connoisseur's gaze at all the masterpieces; you can ski—on paper—with dash and grace down Alpine slopes or pose for entranced photographers on the shores of the Mediterranean—but if your husband won't go with you; if he goes, but longs to be at home ... then you may as well save the fare.'

'In other words, I'll never be happy unless he's happy?'

'Marriage in a nutshell,' said Mrs. Channing.

'But where's my development, my

personality, my separate self?'

'In the nutshell. There's room for it all. But you'll be happy if you'll remember that men don't change much. Women do. Women adapt themselves, and if you think that means that they lose their individuality, you're wrong. Show me a happy marriage and I'll show you a clever woman.'

Christine was silent. Her eyes were on her mother, and Mrs. Channing knew that she was seeing her for the first time as a person and not as a parent.

'You can't tell me you didn't find it dull at times,' she said at last. 'After all, I've lived with Father too.'

'And thought that because you found him heavy, I must find him dull. That's what your sisters thought, and all three of you were wrong. Outsiders can never judge the look of a marriage.'

'Would you call your children outsiders?'

'In this matter, yes. How could it have been dull? I kept a man happy, and comfortable, and faithful and deeply in love with me for nearly thirty years. I had to protect him from people, but I had to fill the house with your friends. I had to let him be quiet, but keep a happy atmosphere in the home. I had to make you all respect him in spite of his slow ways. I had to make you see him as he is: a wonderful husband and father. Dull? No, it wasn't dull. Now you can turn and look out of the window again; they're coming.'

The two men were approaching, but slowly. There were things to be looked at on the way; a man didn't have to have a castle, Mr. Channing was reflecting, before he knew how to make a lawn. Not a sign of a weed anywhere. Weed-killer? Not at all, young man; you could spray till you were blue in the face and when you got up the next morning, you'd still find the things sticking out of your lawn. The thing to do...

'It looks all right,' Christine said, watching them. 'But where does that get us? The hold-up's all on the other side. Finding that James and Father are blood brothers isn't going to get me married, is it?'

'It's going to be a help in the long run. Come outside and join them. Bring that tray of drinks, will you?'

Over beer, the men discussed the niceties of pruning and the problem of pests; Christine's attempts to introduce more general topics were met politely but absently, the conversation then reverting to technicalities. Mr. Channing led James away to show him some trenches that had nothing to do with warfare, and then, bringing him in to lunch, was obliged to surrender him to Christine. When the time came for James to take his leave, Mrs. Channing had some difficulty in convincing her husband that he would prefer to be seen off by Christine alone, and it was with reluctance that he allowed himself to be led away at last and shut inside the house.

James, standing beside his car, rocked Christine to and fro in an embrace that was at once passionate and comforting.

'Darling, don't cry. It'll soon pass.'

'I love you,' sobbed Christine. 'I didn't mean to cry, but it's three whole months.'

James's clasp tightened.

'Don't cry, Christine. I can't bear it when you cry. Try to understand why I'm doing this.'

'I do understand. But three months...'

'We needn't waste them; there's a lot we can do. You can start getting things together for—'

'If you're going to say my trousseau, you needn't. I'm not going to prepare for my wedding until I'm certain it's going to come off.'

He lifted her face and made her meet his eyes.

'Christine, you promised you'd never say that to me.'

'He's got three whole months to work on you. That Katherine...'

'I've known her all my life. I've seen her, on and off, since I was born. Do you suppose she's going to exercise a special fascination all of a sudden? She must be just about as sick of hearing of me as I am of her. I love you and I'm going to marry you—with something to offer you if all goes well, with practically nothing if things go wrong.'

'I wish you'd been somebody else.'

'And that,' James said firmly, 'is where we differ. I like being who and what I am. You're born what you're born. I'm sorry, for your sake, that I'm not going to be able to give you much, apart from a title, but your father and mother have lived happily on less than we're going to have, and they made a go of it. I hope we'll be half as happy, and I hope we'll make half as good parents. Your father . . . You never told me he was a green-fingered wonder.'

'Did you have to waste all that time on our last day talking about potato blight?'

'Who said anything about our last day?'

'It feels like it. You needn't think'—she paused to let him wipe away her tears—'you needn't think I'm going to be the give-all type my mother is.'

'You've got three months to practise in,' he said, and took her gently into his arms and put his lips on hers and kept them there in a desperate attempt to drink in enough sweetness and warmth and passion to tide him over the months of separation. Then he put her from him, got into the car and drove away.

CHAPTER THREE

On deciding to marry James, Christine had given up her secretary's post in London, but not her share of the flat she occupied with a school friend. The unexpected check in her plans left her undecided whether to take another job or to give up the flat and go home.

She returned to London after James's departure and even went so far as to interview a prospective employer, but it seemed to her that James was everywhere; every street brought back memories of him. She knew that he had left the agricultural college, that he had returned to Northumberland, that the chances of meeting him were slight indeed—but the hope still remained and, far from fading, grew at last too strong to be borne. She would, she decided, go home. She would go down to Hampshire, where there were fewer memories of James, where she could move about without this sick feeling of expectation.

But before she had made her arrangements to return, her sisters had closed ranks.

The enforced period of waiting was a matter to be kept within the bounds of the family—but within those confines, the news spread fast. On the Sunday following James's visit, Mr. Channing returned from church to see that his daughter Antoinette had arrived with her husband Max and their two small sons. He had no sooner put the car into the garage than Barbara and her husband rang up from the station to inform him that they had arrived with the baby and required fetching.

Nobody, he thought resentfully, getting out

the car again after a vain attempt to find Max and make him go instead, nobody had asked Barbara and Nigel to come. Nobody had asked Antoinette and Max either. No doubt if Neville and his wife hadn't been abroad, they too would have arrived, luggage and all, as these others had done, to stay the night and give their mother a lot of trouble and to turn the house upside down. He thought suddenly of the two small boys and wished that he had brought them with him; once they got into the garden, who could say what damage they'd do before either of their parents thought of stopping them? Antoinette would pretend she hadn't seen, and Max would pull his hat over his eyes and lean back in his chair and give a good imitation of being asleep.

Mr. Channing did not greatly care for his sons-in-law. He had nothing specific against them and was prepared to allow that they were rather above average in looks and in physique, but both of them seemed to him to have a manner he considered flippant and unfitting, not to say impertinent, in their dealings with him. He couldn't put his finger, he acknowledged when challenged by his wife, on exactly what it was he didn't like, but it was there, just below the surface, and she couldn't say it wasn't. He could stomach them one at a time, but both of them coming down like this, without so much as a by-your-leave, was too much.

He drove the latest arrivals back to the house, and the hour before lunch followed the usual family pattern, with the girls in the kitchen with their mother—doing, their father considered, more talking than helping—and the men in the sunshine on the terrace, drinking beer and keeping an eye on the children.

At lunch, comments on Christine's situation were freely exchanged, Nigel being of the opinion that James had been wrong to agree to the three months' delay and Max, purely to annoy his father-in-law, maintaining that a good many men who had rushed into marriage and fatherhood would have been grateful for a chance to think things over coolly before it was too late. What emerged from all the discussion, to Mr. Channing's surprise, was the fact that Barbara and Antoinette thought their sister the victim of a flint-hearted old autocrat, and had come today with only one end in view: to see that their parents were not going to allow her to languish for the next three empty, waiting months.

After lunch, when the children had been put to rest in the spare room and the grown-ups were drinking their coffee on the terrace, it developed that by parents Barbara and Antoinette meant not parents, but solely their father. Mr. Channing, to his bewilderment and resentment, found himself rapidly manoeuvred into the position of telling an expectant audience what he proposed to do about the matter.

'Do?' he repeated irritably. 'What can anybody do except wait? The thing's settled; they wait three months. What's three months? If they can't wait three months without all this fuss, they oughtn't to—'

'You've missed the point,' Antoinette told him with the air of exaggerated patience that annoyed him so much. 'What we've been saying, Dad, if only you'd listened, was that you can't expect Christine to stay at home for the next three months with nothing to do but brood and think about James and worry about that girl his grandfather's determined to make him marry.'

'Brood? Who said anything about brood?' demanded Mr. Channing angrily. 'She shouldn't have given up her job so soon, but if she feels like brooding, she can find another job, can't she?'

'I saw her yesterday,' said Barbara. 'She looked terrible—pale and drooping. She'd made up her mind to come home, but if she stays here, she'll mope and—'

'There's no need for her to mope,' pointed out Mr. Channing. 'There's plenty to do helping her mother. And I can do with a bit of help in the garden now and then, though none of you ever offered any. Your mother works morning, noon and night—did you ever see her moping?'

'That's quite different,' said Antoinette. 'Do

42

stick to the point, Dad. Christine's got three months in which to imagine James falling in love with that other girl. She'll have no letters from him, no news of him. Stuck up there in Northumberland, she knows nobody who could send her a line now and then to tell her how he's getting on. All she can do is wonder if his beastly grandfather's influence is beginning to work, and if that girl's seeing James day after day. It'll get on her mind, and that's unhealthy.'

'When you and your sister Barbara were engaged,' Mr. Channing reminded her, 'I don't remember seeing Max or Nigel down here day after day.'

'That was partly because we could go up and see them in London whenever we wanted to,' said Antoinette, 'and partly—'

'—and partly,' took up her husband smoothly, 'because the presence of parents during the preliminaries proved prejudicial to the passivity of the prey, pushing him into panic, if not partial or practical paralysis, or to prevarications previous to plunging precipitately from his plight.'

There was a pause.

'Have you finished?' Antoinette enquired coldly.

'Period,' said Max.

'He needs,' said Nigel, 'a punch on his posterior.'

'Will you both kindly shut up?' demanded

43

Antoinette. 'We were talking seriously.'

'Let us then,' said Max, 'proceed with the pow-wow or *pourparler*. Papa is positively purple.'

'Look here,' said their father-in-law, rising, 'I'm not going to sit here wasting my time and listening to a lot of tommy-rot about—'

He was not permitted to leave. There was a move on the part of all the others, so concerted as to stir in him strong suspicions of a plot to make him sit down again.

'What we were coming to,' Antoinette said, 'is that we all think that Christine should go away for a time.'

'Well, what's stopping her?' demanded Mr. Channing. 'If she wants to go away, she can go. I dare say a change of scene wouldn't do her any harm. She could go up and stay with her aunt at Perth for a week or two.'

'We think she ought to *travel*,' said Barbara.

'She can't get to Perth without travelling, can she?' asked Mr. Channing reasonably. 'If she booked a seat on the night train, she'd get up there in time for breakfast. There'd be no need to go to the expense of a sleeper; I went up there once when I was a boy and there was nobody else in the carriage and I was able to stretch out and—'

'*Travel*,' repeated Barbara in a louder voice. 'I do wish you'd listen, Dad. *Travel*. We think Christine ought to go abroad.'

'Well, let her go abroad,' said Mr.

44

Channing. 'It costs money, but that doesn't seem to worry any of you. She won't get any more change staying with that girl she knows in Paris than she would get with her aunt at Perth, but that's her lookout. All the same, you needn't go putting ideas into her head.'

'We're not going to let her sit here for three months, brooding,' said Antoinette. 'She'll be home in a day or two, and what's she coming home to? Nothing! Just watching Mother in the kitchen cooking meals and you pottering about the garden. The only visitors will be one or two decrepit aunts or uncles, or friends that you and Mother have had since Abraham led the Israelites into wherever it was. What sort of life is that?'

'If her home,' said Mr. Channing resentfully, 'doesn't offer any more attraction, I would advise her to—'

'She wants a *change*. She wants a change of scene,' said Barbara in her loudest voice. 'Good heavens, Dad, haven't you got any imagination? She meets James, she falls in love, he falls in love, he goes up to break the good news to his grandfather, she starts thinking about her trousseau—and then what? Nothing! Grandfather wants money and knows where to get it, James agrees to wait three months, and Christine's in the air. She's left alone down here while James has the heiress dangled in front of his nose. Can't you see how Christine must feel? Haven't you ever

45

read about ... about stricken deers?'

'Stricken deers?' echoed the bewildered Mr. Channing. 'What have—'

'Mother!' Barbara turned to appeal to Mrs. Channing. 'Can't you get some sense into his head? Can't you make him understand what we're talking about? His daughter—his youngest and, as we all know, his favourite daughter has taken a bad knock, and what does he do? He sits there and tells her to go and get a job, or stay at home and help you to wash up!'

'She wouldn't be the first,' said Mr. Channing, 'who found a cure in being busy. She—'

'Listen, Father.' Antoinette spoke slowly and clearly, as to the deaf. 'If you don't do something to help her, to distract her, to fill in the next three months, you'll be a pretty poor parent. I've seen her since this thing happened, and so has Barbara. She's in love, and this crazy earl has poked his medieval nose in and made a mess of everything. The least you can do is to see that Christine gets away.'

'I've just said—' began Mr. Channing.

'And you,' ended Antoinette, 'have got to take her.'

Pure astonishment kept her father silent for some moments.

'*Me*?' he brought out at last. '*Me* take her? Take her where?'

'Well, not to Perth,' said Barbara. 'And not

46

to Paris. Somewhere far. Somewhere new. For a cruise.'

Mr. Channing did not at first seem to understand the word.

'A cruise?' he said slowly. 'A *cruise*?'

'A voyage in a vessel,' explained Max, 'to vanquish the vapours.'

'You keep out of this!' Antoinette said, turning on him fiercely. 'Just as we're getting him to the point of actually following what's being said, you go and spoil everything. A cruise,' she proceeded, readdressing her father. 'We think that you and mother ought to come up to London with us tomorrow morning, go to a travel agent and buy tickets for somewhere—somewhere exciting—and then spring it on Christine as a surprise.'

Mr. Channing waited until he could command his breath.

'May I point out,' he said at last, 'that a cruise means going away on a ship? It means several days, if not weeks, spent away from one's home. It means a useless, a senseless expenditure on—on what? A cramped and stuffy cabin, loud and uncongenial fellow-passengers, seasickness, unsuitable food, a drive round some foreign port in which everybody is waiting to rob you—and nothing to show at the end of it but a few trashy trinkets. The only thing to be said in favour of such a silly scheme is the pleasure and relief of getting home again.'

47

'It's obvious,' said Nigel, 'that you haven't read the brochures. If you had, you'd know that you live in suites, dress for dinner every night, dance till dawn, sit on the Captain's right and win the daily Sweep daily.'

'And if you think,' proceeded Mr. Channing, as if nobody had spoken, and addressing both his daughters, 'if you think that a man can walk out—sail out, in fact—leaving a garden like this to itself, you're even sillier than I sometimes feel obliged to acknowledge. Why, if I'm away for—'

'Oh, *pooh!*' Barbara broke in, making it sound a very rude word indeed. 'A few beans and peas, and the agony of having to miss the strawberries. What would happen if you got ill, or died, or suffered from a plague of locusts, or something? Good heavens, what's a *garden*?'

Bitterness prevented her father from telling her. He sat silent, gnawed by the serpent's tooth. That was all they thought of twenty years of hard work in all weathers. That was all they knew or cared about results. That was all that the unceasing, uninterrupted flow of produce had meant to them. Fresh fruits and vegetables in season, flawless, succulent, health-giving, money-saving. Never, in all that time, so much as a potato bought outside. Fruit bottled for the winter, vegetables canned, deep-freezing tried out, pests identified and destroyed, soils tested and treated, hothouses heated, grapes fit for a king's table set before them or picked and sent to them at school, or in their own homes.

In extremity, he invariably looked to his wife for help. His glance sought hers now, only to find that she was looking away from him, staring studiously into the distance. The invisible line, thrown when he was out of his depth, to support him and bring him back to land, to safe waters, was withheld. She was, he realized with a sinking heart, on the side of the enemy. She had gone over to the ranks of his tormentors. She supported—it was incredible, but it was only too clear—this fantastic proposal to go—the very word filled him with helpless apprehension—cruising. She had heard Barbara's cruel question and she had sat there saying nothing, though she must have known how much it hurt him. He was deserted. He was abandoned.

Cornered, he was driven to using his wits.

'Travel of the kind you're talking about,' he said, his voice firm, 'is extremely expensive. Have you any idea, any of you, what even a short cruise would cost?'

They knew, it appeared, to a tenth of a penny. They had, quite by chance, dropped into Thomas Cook's and made enquiries. Here, also quite by chance, in Nigel's pocket, were several possibilities.

'There's a gorgeous one,' Antoinette said, 'which goes to Greece and—'

'*Greece!*' Mr. Channing's voice was almost a

49

squeak. 'Are you mad? Greece! Why not Peru or Kashmir or Timbuctoo and be done with it?'

'You can go,' said Antoinette implacably, 'the whole way, or you could fly to Venice and...'

Her voice died away. Sensible as the project had seemed earlier, united as they all were in a determination to force it upon their father, nobody present could by any last stretch of imagination imagine him flying to Venice. They might as successfully have urged him to be the first grandfather to fly to the moon.

Silence fell on the company—and then, for the first time, Mrs. Channing spoke.

'Greece,' she said quietly, 'is too far for your father.'

The words acted like a tonic on the younger members and like a blight on Mr. Channing. Was that all she could say at last? Greece was too far. What could that mean? It was nothing but an invitation to the others, a clear encouragement to them to continue, but on a slightly less fantastic level.

'I do not,' he said loudly, 'propose to take Christine on any cruise, near or far. In the first place, I cannot and will not leave the garden, especially at this time of the year. Barbara asked what would happen if I did; well, I'll tell you. The lawns would become a wilderness, and the food-stuffs you've all enjoyed for so long, and which have saved you so much money, and kept you and your children well and strong, will come to an end. If you all think I can just step out and cruise round Greece and come back and tackle all the—'

'Hawkins,' interrupted Mrs. Channing, 'will come every day.'

Her husband turned himself round in his chair and stared at her with hope slowly draining out of him. It was a double blow. That she should have leagued herself against him to force him to leave his beloved house and garden was bad enough; that she should have gone so far as to brush aside the principles he had worked so hard to instil into them all, principles of thrift and saving and value-for-money ...

'Have you forgotten,' he asked her, 'what Hawkins charges per day—per hour?'

'He's expensive,' acknowledged Mrs. Channing, 'and so is a cruise, but this is, in a way, an emergency. I don't go as far as to say that Christine will go into a decline if she isn't given a holiday, but I do think that if you and I could take a little trip with her, it would do her good. And do us good. You haven't been away from this house for more than three days during the past I don't know how many years. And—'

'What can any place in the world offer,' he asked, 'that we can't find here at home? What can—'

'And neither,' she ended, 'have I.'

There was a long, tense silence. The words,

quiet, unemphatic, had nevertheless the effect of a bomb on all present. Never in Barbara or Antoinette's lives, never in the knowledge of her two sons-in-law, had Mrs. Channing been heard to say anything that could be taken as criticism, either of her husband or of her way of life. They had regarded her, as they had regarded Mr. Channing, as fixed, immovable, as much a permanent feature of the house as her husband was of the grounds. Attempts to persuade her to visit friends or relations had failed; she had kept open house, entertained her friends and theirs, submitted to their efforts to keep her up to date in dress and speech and ideas—and stayed at home. She went up to London to shop or to go to a theatre, and sometimes stayed overnight; then she was back again. Quiet, fun-loving, in her own way even gay, she had been fixed, content, as long as they could remember. But her words still hung in the air—and the tone in which they had been uttered.

'Good God!' said Mr. Channing at last.

He was lost. If she wasn't going to support him, he would have to look to himself. To sit there and insinuate—more, to state quite openly that he had held her here, a prisoner...

'Oh, for heaven's *sake*,' burst out Barbara in a clumsy attempt at comforting him, 'what's money?'

The question her father could answer unhesitatingly and with a conviction that sprang from the depths of his being. He knew that he was considered by many people a mean man, a close, a penny-pinching man. He cared little about the label, feeling it to be inaccurate and unjustified. Careful he might be in small matters, but the pennies made the shillings and the shillings made the pounds—and in the long run, it was the pennies that counted; that he had counted. In big things he had paid out, paid up—you only had to ask his wife. Had he ever refused to pay, even when he felt the demands excessive? Had he quibbled about his children's education? Hadn't he met all those iniquitous bills from schools whose Bursars must have sat up all night and every night wondering how soon they could raise the fees another twenty guineas or so? Hadn't his son, his daughters always had allowances that had probably been the ruin of them? Hadn't they all always had all the suits and the dresses they needed, and enough pairs of shoes to supply a family of centipedes?

For travel, he was prepared to admit, he had not been disposed to bleed himself white. They were English, born and bred, and he had never tired of reminding them that they had the length and breadth of England to explore. When they'd done that, when they'd seen the Lakes and the Fells, when they'd exhausted all the beauties of the lovely countryside and the historic old towns, then let them come to him and talk about Spain and Italy. If they wanted to roam about foreign lands, they must do so at their own expense.

Until now, they had done so. Until now.

'Travelling without you,' he heard his wife saying, 'would have been no fun. If you couldn't enjoy it, neither could I. But we ought to go now, for Christine's sake. We needn't go far.'

Clutching this lifeline, Mr. Channing got up and made his way miserably to the kitchen garden, and the eyes of his family followed him with expressions varying between tenderness and amazement.

'Incredible,' murmured Nigel. 'You could understand it if it was only money—but it isn't. He just doesn't want to go. Didn't he'—he turned to his mother-in-law—'didn't he ever want to go anywhere?'

'Never,' replied Mrs. Channing tranquilly.

'I suppose,' Max conceded, 'that's the secret of happiness—that old yarn about searching the world for it and finding it on the kitchen doorstep when you got home. But what about broadening the mind, or seeing how the other half live, or shoving one's horns out of the shell once in a while?'

'His work was here, or near here, and his garden gave him more pleasure than anything in the world,' pointed out Mrs. Channing.

'But didn't you want to go?' he asked.

She hesitated.

'I used to try to move him in the early days

54

because I didn't understand him as well as I do now. When I understood him better, I stopped bothering him.'

'But now,' Antoinette asked, 'you think he should go?'

'Yes. He won't go far, but it's his last chance—our last chance—of a bit of family life. If we don't take Christine away, she'll get another job in London; this is a blessed opportunity to see the last of the last of our children.'

'But if he grumbles all the way there and all the way back, it isn't going to be much fun, is it?' Barbara asked.

Her mother smiled.

'He won't grumble out loud; he'll mutter under his breath. I'm just being selfish, I suppose. I wouldn't like to go without him, so—just this once—he's got to come along. It'll shake some fresh ideas into that head of his.'

*   *   *

On the following morning, Mr. Channing saw Hawkins, as unbelieving as himself, summoned as a preliminary to being left in sole charge. He himself, and his wife, were driven by Nigel to the station and there placed on a train in charge of Antoinette and Max, who were to conduct him to the travel agent's and see that he didn't leave until he had planned and paid for a cruise for himself, for his wife

55

and for Christine, on the first ship on which accommodation could be obtained.

Misery kept him dumb all the way to London. He recognized dimly that what he was doing—under duress—was right, if not for his daughter, then for his wife. She had given, for the first time in almost thirty years, a clear indication that she wanted something, and there was no possibility of refusing. But he was being led into what he considered senseless and almost unjustified extravagance, and the thought of the cheque that he would shortly be called upon to write left him feeling faint.

Panic gave him, at the travel agent's, a certain poise and firmness which in turn gave him an advantage over the glossy-haired young man on the other side of the counter, who had at first, Mr. Channing thought, mistaken him for a millionaire. He was able without too much argument to brush aside the Costa Brava (overcrowded); Rome (taken by an aunt as a boy); Sicily (bandits); Corsica, Sardinia, Crete (haven't you got anything but islands?); Spain (bloodthirsty devils); Andorra (who wants to buy stamps?) and the Pyrenees (can't say I care for climbing). At the Fiords, he paused for the first time. This was getting nearer. The nearer, the cheaper.

Brittany. That was nearer still. But you couldn't, the young man said, cruise round Brittany. No? Why not, pray? Well, you could go in your own yacht, if you had one, or you could make an arrangement with one of those private owners who advertised, but he, the young man, wouldn't advise it. They charged a lot, and you never knew what you were in for. Far better to stick to the big shipping companies and choose one of those comfortable ships that called in at Lisbon and then went on to the Mediterranean ports and on to—

Mr. Channing was no longer listening. The word Lisbon had winged its way across the counter, bringing with it not only the hope of a cheap journey but also the memory of an old acquaintance.

'Lisbon,' he said musingly. 'Lisbon. That reminds me.'

Everybody waited.

'I've got it!' Mr. Channing exclaimed, and turned to his wife. 'Wasn't Lisbon the place that old Colonel Bell-Burton went out to? You remember, surely? He married that niece of Canon Crane—forget her name—and came to say good-bye when he'd finished with the Army and was off to live in Lisbon. But no; it wasn't Lisbon. It was somewhere near.'

'Estoril?' suggested the young man.

'No.'

'Setubal? Sesimbra? Cascais?'

'No, no, no.'

'Sintra?'

'That's it! Sintra! That's the place.' Joy and relief broke like dawn and irradiated Mr.

Channing's face. That was the answer. Sintra. There'd be the fares to Lisbon to pay, of course—and back. But Bell-Burton had—

'Don't you remember his asking us to go over and stay with them?' he asked his wife. 'Remember how insistent he was? And he wrote more than once inside Christmas cards telling us they had room for us.'

'That was sixteen years ago,' pointed out Mrs. Channing.

'There is,' put in the young man, 'an excellent hotel just outside Sintra. It's a restored palace and—'

'Palace?' Mr. Channing glared at him suspiciously. 'What do they charge?'

The young man told him.

'Well, that seems reasonable enough,' said Mr. Channing. 'Per week, of course.'

'Per day,' said the young man, down his nose.

'Per... Some mistake,' stated Mr. Channing positively. 'But it doesn't matter. We shall be staying with friends. I shall require a double and a single cabin to Lisbon as soon as possible. Tourist class.'

'First class,' said Antoinette.

'And the same accommodation back to England in two weeks' time,' said Mr. Channing.

'Four weeks,' said Antoinette.

Four weeks ... Four weeks away from his garden ...

He heard, with a sense of reprieve, several heartening sentences being delivered by the young man. One couldn't just *go*; one had to put oneself on the waiting list. Accommodation to Lisbon was almost as difficult as accommodation *from* Lisbon, if you follow me. He would do his best, but he couldn't guarantee anything. He would let them know. Would they require bathrooms?

'No,' said Mr. Channing.

'Yes,' said Antoinette. 'And outside cabins, looking on to a deck if possible. A. or B. deck; nothing in the bowels, naturally. And ... You will try, won't you?'

Her smile, suddenly unleased, sent the blood to her husband's head and licked hotly round the glossy-haired young gentleman on the other side of the counter. Mr. Channing paid a deposit and was led out, his thoughts whirling between shame at his daughter's low form of attack, sick dread at the expense it would probably lead him into, pride in her beauty, disgust at her exhibition and pity for her husband, who now wouldn't be able to give his mind to his work.

He followed his wife into the first Hampshire-bound train and gave voice to his hopes.

'Not likely,' he said, 'that they'll be able to fit in three passengers at the last moment at this time of year. You heard that fellow say how full everything was?'

59

Mrs. Channing said nothing. Her mind was on Antoinette, and on Antoinette's smile. They would get berths. They would also get bathrooms. They would be on A. or B. deck and they would not have inside cabins.

There was no doubt, she reflected, that Antoinette—like herself—had an excellent sense of timing.

CHAPTER FOUR

For the next three days, Mr. Channing lived in hope. There was no word from the travel agent, who had, he remembered, held out very little prospect of passages. Their names would be placed on the waiting list, and after a time he would demand the return of his deposit and Christine and her mother could go up to Perth for a nice change.

On the fourth day, however, a bulging envelope appeared on his plate at breakfast. Examining its contents, he learned to his dismay that a first-class double cabin for himself and his wife, and a first-class cabin for his daughter, both with bathrooms, had been booked on *S.S. Monmouth*, sailing for Lisbon at the end of the week. Passengers would embark at Southampton or join the boat train leaving from Waterloo at 5 p.m. on Saturday. The bill for the balance of the fares was enclosed; an early, not to say immediate, cheque would oblige.

'It's a mistake,' said Mr. Channing, when his breath returned. 'You wouldn't have to pay that to get to Australia and back!'

'Yes, you would, Bruce.'

His wife's voice was quiet, but something in it told him that the time for argument was past. He finished his breakfast without enjoyment and then went to his desk and wrote a cheque. His wife blotted it and bore it away, to be enclosed with a letter of acceptance, written by herself, to the travel agent.

For the next few days Mr. Channing, standing bewildered on the bank, watched flowing past him a river of excited daughters, interfering sons-in-law, out-of-date passports, unfamiliar dinner-jackets, new ties and shirts, travellers' cheques, ticket folders and embarkation cards. He was photographed, he was made to try on trousers with too-tight waistbands, he was made to sign and sign again. He saw money, hard-earned, jealously guarded, flowing past with the rest.

He had composed, with his wife's aid, a reply-paid telegram to Colonel Bell-Burton; they were coming, it said; they would be grateful to be put up while inexpensive accommodation was being sought. A reply, polite but brief, came from the Colonel: he looked forward to seeing them.

The ceaseless activity of the week ended in

the moment of departure. They were going. Mrs. Channing walked round the house for the last time; Hawkins stood on the lawn, cap in hand, receiving final instructions. The taxi came to the door, the luggage with its bold labels was carried out. They were on their way.

There was nobody at the station to see them off, since with great forethought, Nigel had applied to the shipping office and had obtained four passes to board the *Monmouth*. Mr. Channing, leaning in a daze over the rail of the first-class deck and trying to make himself believe that he had embarked, saw his two married daughters and their husbands hurrying up the gangway in the happy certainty of being able to dine on board before the ship left. The family made their way to what Mr. Channing thought was simply the sheltered end of the deck but which proved to be a verandah café; no sooner were they seated than a waiter materialized at his elbow and asked what they would like to drink. The order was given, the drinks brought and the charge sheet placed before Mr. Channing. He signed it with reluctance and then led the way down to the dining-saloon, where he was obliged, after several evasive answers, to admit to an inquisitive steward that only three out of the party of seven were passengers.

Darkness had fallen as they dined; when they went up on deck to take leave of the visitors, the unfamiliar lounges, the discreetly-lit, long, narrow, featureless corridors struck a chill to Mr. Channing's heart. Cold and cheerless as the quay looked, with its sheds yawning black and empty, he would have given much to have been standing on it watching the ship depart. He heard the blast of the siren and saw the dark waters dividing ship from shore. Bells sounded, engines began to throb; the *Monmouth* had put to sea.

Mrs. Channing soon went down to the cabin which, though not cramped, did not allow much freedom of movement for two. Her husband stayed on deck for a time, watching the ship gliding past the dark, dimly-lit shapes of other vessels and heading relentlessly towards the Channel. He went down to bed at last, found his wife asleep, and undressed with a cold feeling of inevitability: he was here and he would have to go through with it.

On the following morning, he walked the deck between his wife and daughter. The wind was fresh and the sea danced with small, playful waves. Later, the waves grew too big to be playful, and at tea in the lounge, Mrs. Channing not being present, Christine poured out her father's tea. At dinner, Mr. Channing found himself alone; he ate well and went for a walk on deck afterwards. When at last he went down to his cabin, it was to find his wife lying on her own bed and his daughter lying on his. She was in her nightdress, curled up into a ball with her back turned to a world which at present held no attractions for her.

'Feeling queer?' her father asked unnecessarily.

She made no reply, but from the other bed came a sound that might have been a moan. Mr. Channing turned towards it.

'Can't think what knocked you off your feet,' he said. 'The sea's not too bad. Pretty to watch; lot of white horses heaving up and down and—'

'Go away,' said his wife.

He hardly heard the whisper, so faint was it, but what came through clearly enough was a note of menace. Bewildered, he turned back to his daughter.

'Better get back to your own cabin,' he advised. 'I'd like to turn in.'

'Go away,' said Christine.

'Eh?'

'Go *away!*'

Still addressing the curve of her shoulder, he began a heated protest.

'Look here, I'm sorry you're down to it, though for the life of me I can't see why. The ship'—it made a plunging movement and Mr. Channing clutched the wardrobe for support—'the ship's moving a bit, but you're at sea, after all; must expect a bit of pitch and toss and—'

'Jump overboard,' requested Christine.

'Eh?'

She turned with a sudden, fierce movement.

Her eyes, red-rimmed in a pale green, unfamiliar countenance, rested on him with loathing.

'I said jump overboard.'

'But look here—you're in my bed!'

He was once more addressing her shoulder. He turned to his wife to find her lying with eyes closed and a look of such suffering on her face that he did not dare to speak to her. After standing for some time in indecision, he appealed to Christine.

'I've got to go to bed, haven't I?' he pointed out.

He saw her plunge a hand beneath the pillows. She dragged out his pyjama jacket, groped again and found his trousers. Without turning, she held them out, and he took them.

'Go away,' she said.

He looked at the two recumbent forms and decided not to say that this was what came of cruising. He went out, walked down a long corridor and found Christine's cabin and went in, hoping as he did so that nobody would see him coming out of it in the morning and mistake him for somebody else's father.

He had brought his razor, his bath towel and a change of clothes. Shutting the cabin door and looking about him, he looked in vain for a place to put them. On the dressing-table was day cream, night cream, beauty cream, deep beauty cream, cleansing lotion, deep cleansing lotion, eau de Cologne, face powder, talcum powder, lipsticks, hair brush and comb, hand mirror, two photographs of James, one of himself and his wife, a jewel case, tissues, hair lotion and a box of cigarettes. There were dresses on the bed and over the chair; a dressing-case rested on the stool.

He went into the bathroom and placed his belongings on pegs and stool and small marble shelf. Then he undressed, got into bed and fell instantly asleep.

He was awakened by an unaccustomed sound and an unaccustomed sight—the creaking of timbers as the ship rolled heavily, and a stewardess setting tea and fruit and a news-sheet beside him. He sat up hurriedly and then cowered below the covers.

'I am Miss Channing's father,' he explained. 'My daughter stayed with her mother last night; they were not feeling well.'

'Half the passengers are off their feet, sir,' the stewardess told him. 'When we get into the Bay, the other half'll go down. It doesn't make any difference to the long-distance passengers; they've time enough to get their sea legs. It's these Lisbon ones I'm sorry for. If you're a bad sailor, I always say, why go by sea and spend three days in bed on dry biscuits and beef tea? It's a waste of money, for one thing.'

She went out and closed the door, leaving Mr. Channing staring at it bleakly; out of his party of three, two were showing every sign of remaining off their feet and on beef tea and

66

biscuits.

He knocked gently on the door of his cabin on his way to breakfast. In response to a moan, he went in. One glance told him that neither his wife nor his daughter was in any mood for conversation. He left them and went up on deck warm with indignation at the idea of a shipping company's charging passengers for food they couldn't eat. It was rank robbery.

By the time he went down to the saloon for breakfast, his walk in the fresh, boisterous air had given him appetite enough for his own meal and resolution enough to eat his wife's and Christine's. Looking about him as he ate, he noted that only half a dozen other passengers were present.

His own indifference to the movement of the ship, which his staggering progress back to the deck told him was increasing, gave him a feeling of surprise and mild triumph. He saw a few people on deck, but most of them were lying under rugs on deck-chairs, looking stricken. One or two walked briskly round the deck and it became more and more difficult for Mr. Channing, on passing and repassing them, to avoid the exchange of greetings. He therefore decided to go to the deck above, which, owing to its lack of shelter, he might expect to have to himself.

It looked, at first, deserted—and then he saw, at the far end, the figure of a woman. Beyond her were some kennels; beside her were two magnificent young Great Danes, leashed, but bounding excitedly and entangling themselves in their leads. As Mr. Channing approached, he saw that the woman was elderly—between sixty-five and seventy—and of large build. She was tall, broad-shouldered and what he termed full-figured. She wore a tweed coat that flapped and beat violently round her calves; her hair was confined in a net over which was tied a white gauze veil. Braced against the wind, pausing to steady herself at each swing of the ship, she made, with the two dogs, an impressive picture. As he drew near, Mr. Channing saw that her features were heavy but handsome and that she had a proud, even a haughty air.

It was only possible to walk on one side of the deck, access to the other being barred by canvas-covered piles of deck-chairs which would, no doubt, be set out when the ship reached calmer waters. There was nothing to do but walk to and fro, and soon the woman and the dogs were passing and repassing him within the bounds set for the exercising of animals. There was no need, however, for Mr. Channing to worry about any exchange of greetings; the stranger's gaze, whenever they neared one another, remained fixed on a point just above his head, and something in their expression told Mr. Channing that anything below that point was unworthy of her notice.

Old style, thought Mr. Channing

admiringly, seeking shelter at last. The sort of carriage you didn't see nowadays. Pride. Presence. Up there in all that wind, with two spirited dogs to handle, and not a particle of dignity lost. No fuss, no dishevelment, none of this staggering and slipping towards the scuppers that was affecting everybody, including himself. Foreign, of course; you could see that at once. Rather like those pictures of Russian women—strong features and a Slav look. Be interesting to know where she was going; probably, like most of the passengers, she was bound for a South American port. She had a distinctly well-to-do look; she might own one of those big ranches out there. It was easy enough to picture her as the head of a great estate.

Putting the interesting stranger out of his mind, Mr. Channing applied himself to the business of passing the day. He made frequent trips to his cabin, but was not made welcome. He found the library open, thought of taking out a book, thought of not taking out a book. He examined various large maps and saw little flags marking the ship's position. He wandered through the deserted public rooms, went into the almost empty bar and ordered a beer, went for another walk and with deep relief heard the gong sound for lunch. Going down, he found only six passengers at their places; one of them was the woman who had been exercising the dogs.

On his next visit to the cabin, Mr. Channing saw that his wife and daughter had drunk some beef tea, but had left the dry biscuits untouched. They were both asleep. Tip-toeing out, he caught sight of a booklet which he recognized as the passenger list, and took it up to the lounge with him. Glancing through it, he decided that there were several foreign names which could have fitted the dog-woman, but the most likely was that of the Baronesa Narvão. Her destination was Lisbon.

By the time the dinner gong sounded, even Mr. Channing had to admit that the sea was very rough indeed, but a slight feeling of unease was overcome by his determination to deprive the shipping company of further profit. Going down to the saloon, he was interested to be given his plate of soup inside protective wooden barriers that had been placed on the tables. The meal was punctuated by sounds of crashing crockery as one or other of the stewards was caught by a sudden lurch of the vessel. Mr. Channing ate, and across the vast empty spaces of the saloon, met the eyes of his fellow diners and was surprised to find himself sending and receiving friendly signals. It was as if he was with comrades; a member of a brotherhood to which he had had no idea he belonged: that of the order of good sailors.

There was a movement near the large double doors, and he saw the dog-owner coming in. She looked regal in a long, graceful black gown; jewels winked at her throat and wrists. Two stewards sprang to assist her to her place; she accepted the help of one, waved the other away and timed her footsteps to the rise and fall of the ship, achieving a remarkable degree of steadiness. She sat down, and her eyes swept haughtily round the saloon; to Mr. Channing's astonishment and gratification, they rested for a brief moment on himself, and there was graciousness enough in the glance to cause him to lift himself off his seat in the semblance of a bow. He wanted to go at once to the cabin and talk to Madeleine about this strange culmination to a strange day—but Madeleine was asleep, and he had only had soup and fish; there was still the duckling he had ordered, and ice-cream, and fruit, with coffee up in the lounge afterwards; he had paid for it; he might as well have it.

On deck the next morning, there was no question of passing without a bow. The dogs paused to press against his legs, and he patted their magnificent heads.

'You are fond of dogs?'

The question was uttered in a loud, rather harsh voice, and in a strong foreign accent, but Mr. Channing, who had always declared that a soft voice was a woman's greatest asset, felt that here were assets enough. A handsome woman indeed; a pity, he thought, that Madeleine wasn't here to see.

'Yes,' he said, 'I'm very fond of them. As

71

long,' he added to himself, 'as they don't run riot in my garden.'

'You are an authority?'

'No—oh, by no means; no,' he hastened to disclaim.

'I am,' she announced. 'I am well known as an authority. These'—she indicated the Great Danes—'are champions.'

'Yes, I can see that,' said Mr. Channing. 'How long have you had them?'

'Had them? They are not mine. I am taking them to Portugal for a friend.'

Mr. Channing gave her a look of surprise and respect. Up here every morning in this wind, on a sea like this, exercising two spirited animals—for a friend.

'That's very kind of you,' he said.

'Kind? Yes, it is kind!' She shrugged—a prolonged, expressive movement Mr. Channing thought charming. 'But for one's friends one is kind, no?'

'Not always, I'm afraid.'

'In my case, always. If you ask everybody, what will they tell you? The Baronesa, they will say, will do anything for her friends. The Baronesa Narvão. You are who?'

Mr. Channing told her, and explained that his wife and daughter were indisposed.

'It is stupid,' observed the Baronesa, contempt in her tone, 'to come in a ship if you cannot enjoy to travel on a ship. The sea will not always be calm; everybody knows this,

72

isn't it? The Bay of Biscay is known. Even if it is calm on top, underneath there will be disturbance. To pay so much, and to see nothing but the walls of your cabin—what is there in this? It is very stupid.'

To agree would have seemed a reflection on his wife and daughter; Mr. Channing patted the dogs.

'You go to Lisbon?' enquired the Baronesa.

'Well, a bit farther on, as a matter of fact. We're going to a place called Sintra.'

'Sintra?' She smiled—a disappointment to Mr. Channing, since her smile was unattractive, and robbed her face of a good deal of its beauty. 'That is extraordinary. I myself live at Sintra.'

'Oh, do you really? How ... we ... a coincidence,' mumbled Mr. Channing, wishing, not for the first time in his life, that he had learned to converse without making a fool of himself. 'Permanently?'

'For twenty-two years. I came to Portugal a refugee, hunted from my own country. I came without friends, without money—but I was known, and people came to my assistance. I married a Portuguese; he is dead, but still I remain. I love my home, so why should I move? Only, as now, when friends ask me for something, I leave my house. They could not come themselves to England to get the dogs. Go, Cielle, they begged me—that is my name. So I went to England. I stayed only two weeks;

73

I do not care for England.'

'Oh, don't you? That's extraordinary. I myself—'

'Or for the English. Sometimes, as in the case of yourself, one feels that one is able to make an exception. Where are you going to stay in Sintra?'

'Well, things aren't quite definite yet,' explained Mr. Channing. 'I have a friend there who—'

'What is the name of this friend?'

'He's a fellow called Bell-Burton. I knew him—'

'Bellburton?'

'With a hyphen.'

'I do not,' said the Baronesa, her tone chilly, 'know any Bell-Burton.'

She gave a slight inclination of the head, and resumed her walk. Mr. Channing, dismissed, made his way to lower regions and wished very much that he had not dragged in Colonel Bell-Burton. There had been no need to name names ... but, of course, she'd asked outright. It would be a pity if not knowing the Bell-Burtons made her feel that she ought to know where she was before becoming more friendly.

After dinner, which he enjoyed, Mr. Channing sat alone in the lounge. The Baronesa, coming in shortly afterwards, seated herself on a near-by sofa, and by a wave of her arm invited him to take the chair beside it. Mr. Channing joined her and shortly learned that

74

she liked her coffee black, with brandy. He ordered the brandy and was too late to prevent the steward from bringing two.

'If you do not wish for it,' the Baronesa said, 'I will drink it for you. It is good when one is travelling. Your friends, these Bell-Burtons,' she went on when Mr. Channing had signed the bill—'how long have they been in Portugal?'

'Sixteen years, more or less.'

'So long? But it is not strange that I have not heard of them. I do not care to know many people. I have my own selected friends. How long do you mean to stay?'

'About a month. It depends on when we can get berths on a homeward-going boat.'

'And you mean to stay with this friend?'

'Only while we look round and find a place that suits us.'

'You have not yet made reservations?'

'No. We—'

'But this is something that you should have done long ago—months ago.' She pursed her lips doubtfully. 'Without reservations, at this time of the year ... Perhaps in some hotels, but I do not think that you would like to take your wife and daughter to them. So often, it is the same: I meet people like yourself, charming people, who say that they are going to Sintra. To what place in Sintra? I ask them. They tell me, and inside me—here—I shudder. But what can I say to them? It is by then too late. But in your case, it is not too late. Before you decide anything, you must let me advise you. In this way, you will not be throwing away your money. Money is not to be thrown away.'

Mr. Channing, deeply moved, agreed that it was not. He would, he said, consult the Baronesa before committing himself.

'You will find me always at my house. It is called the Quinta de Narvão. If you ask the way, you say simply Quinta de Narvão and they will direct you. It is well known. It is very beautiful. It is spoken of in all the guide books and all the travel books, but photographs I will not allow. Always I refuse. And now'—she rose—'I will go to my stateroom. Soon the voyage will be over, and I shall thank God. I do not care for travelling, and these cabins are uncomfortable and the food is bad and the service terrible. But it will not be long. I hope your wife and your daughter will soon be well.'

Owing to the storm that blew up in the night and the high seas that raged until the ship entered the Tagus, Mrs. Channing and Christine and the great majority of the passengers emerged, pale and shaken, only when Lisbon was within sight. The air and the sunshine revived them, and the Baronesa, handsome and imposing in a dark blue linen suit with white hat and gloves, stopped as she passed them on deck and, after Mr. Channing had performed an introduction, attempted to revive them further.

'At least you are able to see Lisbon coming near, which is a pretty sight,' she told them. 'But for those who, like yourselves, suffer so much, I always think that another way to travel is best: a train, or an aeroplane. That way, when you arrive, you present to your friends who come to meet you a better appearance, isn't it? Sometimes when I come to meet my friends who have come on a ship, I say to myself: My God, I would not care to arrive like this, a husk, a shell, an apparition to frighten. Your friends will be here to receive you?'

'Sure to be,' said Mr. Channing, searching the quay towards which the ship was moving.

'I have been saying to your husband,' the Baronesa told Mrs. Channing, 'that as I live at Sintra and know it better than anybody, he must ask me before deciding which place you shall go to. It is easy to be deceived. I said to him that of course you should have booked already, but if it is all full, you need not worry. If there is difficulty, you must come to me and I will help you.'

Mrs. Channing expressed her gratitude for this kindness.

'It is nothing.' The Baronesa waved a hand. 'Already your husband and I are friends. He and I, and only one or two others, have not been indisposed on this voyage. With me, it is always the same: the sea, rough or smooth, does not make a difference. I arrive as now, refreshed.'

She bowed and left them, and Christine looked after her resentfully.

'I arrive, as now, a husk, a shell, an apparition to frighten,' she said. 'She's short on tact, but all the same, what she said was right: for those who suffer so much, another way of travel is best. Dad can take my name off the waiting list for a return passage.'

Mr. Channing was not listening. The ship was gliding slowly past the approaches to Lisbon, and he could see a wide, shady riverside road and, beyond, a stretch of public garden which took his mind back to the blooms he had left at home. A gardener dragged a hose from bed to bed, directing a glittering shower of water over the plants and making Mr. Channing's nostrils quiver with the remembered smell of warm wet earth.

His wife recalled him.

'I think I can see Colonel Bell-Burton,' she said. 'Over there by the crane.'

'Can't be,' Mr. Channing said, after a long look. 'It's like him in a way, but older.'

'Sixteen years older,' his wife reminded him.

They stayed on deck long enough to establish that it was indeed the Colonel; then they went below to see about the last of the packing, and the formalities of landing. When at last they had disembarked and passed through the Customs shed, the Colonel hurried up to greet them. He was a short, stout man, deeply tanned, with a broad face under a white

Panama hat, and a fussy manner. He held out his arms as though to embrace all three Channings, and then, seizing Mr. Channing's hand, pumped it up and down vigorously.

'Splendid to see you again, Bruce; welcome, welcome. Couldn't make you out at first up there on deck; chap's aged, I said to myself. Funny how one forgets to count the years. Well, Madeleine? Nice to see you again. And my word! how young Barbara's shot up! No? Antoinette? *No? Can't* be little Christine? Well, well, well, that shows you, doesn't it?'

'How are you and Thelma?' enquired Mrs. Channing.

'We're fine, fine—but as a matter of fact, you've just happened to come at an awkward time for us. Didn't like to say anything in my telegram for fear of sounding putting-off, but the fact is that we can't put you up. My daughter—I dare say you don't remember her—came out here and married a Dutchman who's in business in Lisbon, and they're just off to Holland for a month and Thelma and I are having the three children and their nurse to stay with us out at Sintra until their parents get back. I'm on my way to the airport to see them off now, as a matter of fact—plane goes in an hour. Thelma's at home with the children, but she sent you her love.' The Colonel took off his hat, wiped his brow and put his hat on again. 'Been a bit of a business fixing it all up.'

'I hope we haven't—' began Mrs. Channing.

'Oh, no, no, no! Splendid to see you all,' declared the Colonel. 'Only sorry you came just when the house was cram-jam. I've fixed you all up at a little place quite near us; place called the Pensão Pombal. Small, nothing grand, but clean. It wasn't easy to find anything; tourists flooding the place.'

'We're very grateful to you,' said Mrs. Channing.

'Pleasure, pleasure. Afraid I can't take you out there, though,' said the Colonel. 'Don't want to miss seeing the plane go off. I've made a deal with a taxi driver—he's on the look-out for you. He'll run you to the Pensão for two hundred escudos, or three-fifty if you need two cars. He talks a bit of English and he knows where to go.' He paused for a hurried handshake all round. 'You'll forgive me if I rush off? I'll try and look in on you this evening; if not, tomorrow. 'Bye for now; splendid to see you all again.'

He backed away, Panama held aloft; then he put it on again and returned to say something more.

'Don't be put off by the first look at the Pombal; it's not a bad place. The food might be a bit rough, but they've promised to look after you. The water's safe, but you can get the bottled kind if you'd rather.'

He took off his hat once more, moved a few steps backward, collided with a porter, narrowly missed falling headlong over the

Channings' luggage, and then turned and threaded a way through the crowd. The Channings made their way out to the road, located the taxi but were held up for a time by Mr. Channing's refusal to admit that three passengers and their luggage could not all fit into it. The argument, on the driver's side voluble and passionate, on Mr. Channing's a simple but firm repetition of the words Taxi-One, reinforced by an upheld forefinger, was resolved in an unexpected manner. From the innumerable waiting cars, one presently slid silently out—a long, sleek, chauffeur-driven vehicle that Christine, bored with the hold-up and giving her attention to the passing scene, watched for a few moments before recognizing its occupant. Then she spoke in a good imitation of the Colonel's manner.

'Well, well, well, look what we've got here. Father's girl friend.' She pulled her father's coat sleeve. 'Turn round,' she directed. 'She wants to get a long, farewell look at you.'

The Baronesa was doing more than looking. She had ordered the car to stop. A manservant seated beside the chauffeur left the vehicle to walk across and address himself, cap in hand, to Mr. Channing.

'If you have no room for all your luggage, Senhor, the Senhora Baronesa will put some into her car.'

The car edged nearer and Mr. Channing addressed the Baronesa through the window which she had let down.

'It's really very good of you,' he said, 'but we couldn't dream—'

'Two suitcases I will take,' said the Baronesa. 'If this will help you—'

'It would solve everything,' Mr. Channing told her.

Two large suitcases were swallowed up with ease in the luggage compartment of the car.

'To what address,' the Baronesa asked, 'shall they be sent?'

'Well, I'll have to ask the taxi driver,' said Mr. Channing. 'He knows the name, but I'm afraid I—'

'Do not trouble,' the Baronesa said. 'When you arrive you must send me a message and I will have your luggage taken to you.'

The car drove away and the Channings were left to their green-and-black taxi. The ship, the quay and the crowds were left behind and soon they were driving along a coast road which Mr. Channing, after a time, announced from his seat beside the driver to be as fine and as picturesque as any he had ever seen.

'Just before we pin on the rosette,' Christine said, 'tell us what you've seen.'

'You don't have to travel in order to know what places look like,' her mother pointed out. 'Stop teasing your father and sit back and get the feel of Portugal.'

With a map bought from Boots the Chemist spread upon his knee, Mr. Channing followed their progress until they turned towards the abrupt, sharp-pointed range of hills on which Sintra stood. The road twisted, straightened, twisted again; they began to climb, and were soon driving along narrow, tree-shaded lanes or between high walls surrounding large properties. The air was noticeably cooler than it had been when they left the ship. The taxi slowed down on a horse-shoe turn and they saw before them the Palace of Sintra, with groups of tourists going up or down the steps or sitting at tables in front of roadside cafés.

'Nice,' commented Christine. 'I'm glad I didn't stay at home and go into a decline.'

'Poets,' said Mrs. Channing, 'wrote about this place.'

'I'm waiting,' Christine said.

'Well, Byron, for one. But he was a Lusophobe.'

'*Mother!* Can you spell it, too?'

'If you mean he disliked Portugal, why can't you say so?' demanded Mr. Channing. 'I don't care for these phobes and philes.'

'Byron was a Lusophobe but a Sintraphile,' said Christine. 'He said this was the most delightful village in Europe. He obviously,' she ended, looking with distaste at the road into which the taxi was turning, 'didn't see this part of it.'

They were in a narrow, winding lane that ran between low, damp, moss-grown walls; branches of trees met overhead, giving a twilight atmosphere. The road surface alternated between puddles and potholes, and from time to time the walls gave way to depressed-looking little hovels outside which brown-skinned children played.

'If this,' Mr. Channing said slowly, 'is the kind of thing the Colonel thinks we're going to—'

He stopped. The taxi had negotiated a narrow corner and the lane came to an end in thick pine forest. To their left they saw a large, square, open courtyard, and into this the taxi turned, stopping before a small, pale pink house which, in blue letters splashed across a wall, proclaimed itself to be the Pensão Pombal.

For some moments—so great was the change from the damp, dark lane—the Channings sat without moving. Before them was a blaze of colour which, come upon without warning, had an effect almost blinding. The upper windows of the house were half hidden behind trails of bougainvilia that hung from a roof of tiles weathered to pale gold. The railing of the wooden verandah that ran the length of the house, interrupted only by a flight of four wooden steps in the centre, was lost in a tangle of roses—yellow, red, pink and white. Scarlet geraniums lined the steps, pink geraniums cascaded down a low wall on the left. Lining the verandah were more geraniums in pots painted violent shades of purple and green. The plants, the flowers grew as they would; nothing was trained, nothing tended, nothing cut back. The whole effect was one of riotous, triumphant colour.

The doors on the ground floor stood open, giving a glimpse of a black-and-white tiled hall, small, bare, shabby rooms and the pine forest beyond. On one side of the courtyard stood a row of low wooden outhouses, the home of chickens, a donkey, rabbits, geese, turkeys, two large, lean dogs and countless cats; some of these were shut up, others roamed free. Close by was a washing tank and a clothes line hung with garments.

The women of the house were busy. Rooms were being swept, rugs shaken, clothes washed. The only man in sight seemed to be at leisure; he was seated at one of the little iron tables set out along the verandah; as the taxi stopped, he cleared his throat and spat neatly over the railing.

'Before I leave here,' Christine said, 'I'll make him teach me how to do that. Come on, Dad; let's get inside. Something tells me I'm going to like this place.'

Mr. Channing, getting slowly out of the taxi, looked doubtful.

'It's ... well, it's not quite what I ...'

'I like the look of it,' Mrs. Channing said. 'It looks like a home.'

They were getting a warm welcome. The man on the verandah had risen and was

85

shouting for Josefina, Maria-Jose, Maria-Helena and Maria-Innocencia. From the central door came a stout, smiling woman, drying her hands on her apron. The man came up to the taxi, thumped the driver on the back and pushed him towards the back of the house and refreshment. He was between forty and forty-five, short and powerful-looking; he was wearing a checked shirt and serviceable-looking trousers. He hauled out the luggage and gave it to three muscular-looking girls and then looked expectantly at Mr. Channing.

Mr. Channing was unable to say anything, but a friendly instinct led him to put out a hand. It was taken and shaken, and a flood of voluble Portuguese made him welcome. Encircled, shooed like valuable geese towards the house, the Channings were ushered inside.

Mrs. Channing gave a swift, experienced glance round the hall, the uncarpeted staircase, the dark little reception room and a dining-room in which were small tables spread with blue-checked cloths. Clean. All spotless. She gave a soundless sigh of relief. Mr. Channing, sniffing suspiciously for food smells, could detect only floor polish. It all looked plain but good, he thought; if the food was up to scratch, they would do better to stick it out here rather than move to a place no better but far more expensive.

They were taken up to their rooms. Mr. and Mrs. Channing were shown into a small

86

chamber, to enter which it was necessary to shuffle round a vast double bed which took up most of the floor space. Christine had a room like a large-sized cupboard. Both rooms had windows which opened on to the branches of trees; there was presumably a view, for this, the back of the house, hung over a hillside so steep that it seemed unlikely that any other building could block the outlook, but nothing could be seen through the thickly-clustering trees.

They were led downstairs to the verandah and placed round a table on which wine had been set. The large man, who knew no English, stood before them and managed to make them understand that his name was Gustavo and his wife was called Josefina. They had—he held up the necessary number of fingers—nine daughters. Girls, girls, always girls, he told them with no sign of regret. Three were married; another—there she was at the washing tank; her name was Maria de Fatima—was to be married very soon. The next three were called Maria-Jose, Maria-Helena and Maria-Innocencia, who were fifteen, thirteen and eleven respectively and who helped their mother in the house. The remaining two were not yet old enough to be useful.

How a house so small could accommodate a family so large while still leaving room for guests, was not explained. What was clear enough was the family's pleasure in entertaining the visitors and their desire to do everything they could to make them comfortable. Was everything, Gustavo enquired, to their liking?

Everything was. Christine, full of wine and sunshine, only needed James to be quite content. Mrs. Channing, followed by Maria-Jose, Maria-Helena and Maria-Innocencia, went upstairs to unpack. Mr. Channing looked at the wild, rioting flowers and wished that he had thought of packing a pair of secateurs.

Lunch was served in the dining-room at half past one. The meal consisted of thick vegetable soup, fish cooked with rice, veal fried in breadcrumbs, tender green beans, new potatoes and peas, two or three interesting new cheeses, and fruit. The plates were thick and unwarmed and the food, served by three of the girls, was spread out artistically on long, flat dishes and had lost in the arranging most of its heat, but no fault could be found with the quantity or the quality or the standard of cleanliness. It was agreed over coffee on the verandah that the Colonel had chosen well.

The question of fetching the suitcases was raised an hour or so later. Attempts to explain the situation to Gustavo having met with little success, Mr. Channing decided that the best thing to do would be to go for a walk, locate the Quinta de Narvão, thank the Baronesa for her kindness, inform her where they were staying and ask her to write a line or two which they could show their landlord, instructing him to send for the cases.

They set out at about four o'clock and walked slowly up the lane and made their way to the square opposite the Palace. Here they chose a café and stopped to have tea. Once more on their way, they strolled without haste up the pleasant, tree-lined roads and at last stopped to ask a passer-by the way to the Quinta de Narvão.

The house seemed to have the fame its owner had claimed for it. Without hesitation, the man pointed. Up there.

They followed the direction indicated. The road was steep, and on their right was a high, apparently unending wall. Then suddenly, they rounded a corner and came to an enormous, beautifully wrought iron gate. Intricate as was its design, its name could be seen clearly, interlaced with a skill that drew murmurs of admiration from Mr. Channing.

Visible through the gate was a garden with colours as bright and as varied as those at the Pensão Pombal, but here experts had planned and artists had planted. Mr. Channing, gazing in delight, thought that he had never seen flowers displayed with such profusion and such perfection. His eyes roamed from familiar plants to those new to him: an orchestra whose instruments were little blue horns, large scarlet trumpets, pale yellow bells.

Before they could ring the great bell that

hung above the gate, they saw a car coming towards them from the direction of the house. A man appeared and opened the gate; the car came on and the Channings stood aside, only to find it stopping abreast of them. The Baronesa leaned forward.

'Ah, so you have found my house! That is very nice. I was about to go out, but now I shall not. You shall come inside and then I shall learn where you are staying. I shall get out and walk back with you; come.'

The chauffeur sprang out and opened the door; Mr. Channing assisted the Baronesa to alight. Slowly and not without state, they walked together up the drive, the car following them. Like a funeral, thought Christine, only the wrong way round.

The richness, the formal beauty of the garden had been some preparation for the first sight of the house. It stood on a slope, framed by the green of pine woods, tall, pale, pillared, so lovely in the late sunlight that Mrs. Channing gave a murmur of admiration.

'It is lovely, yes,' agreed the Baronesa. 'People think that it is too large for me, but I like to have a great deal of space; why should one cramp oneself?'

She led them up a flight of steps into a marble-floored hall. They walked along thickly carpeted corridors and through a large, beautifully furnished drawing-room, but the Baronesa did not pause until she reached the long doors at the end and ushered the visitors on to a wide, flower-lined terrace.

'Here,' she said, waving a hand towards luxurious garden chairs, 'we shall have tea.'

Mrs. Channing hastened to assure her that they had already had tea and, far from wishing to prevent her from going out, had meant only to make arrangements for the recovery of their luggage.

'But we shall sit for you to rest, isn't it?' the Baronesa rejoined. 'If not tea, then I am sure you would enjoy one of my special little cool drinks. Arturo'—a servant seemed to materialize from behind the balustrade—'will bring some to try.'

Arturo, bowing and going away, returned with a silver tray on which were frosted tumblers half-filled with a honey-coloured liquid.

'Sugar you must have—one lump only,' directed the Baronesa. 'And one only thin slice of lemon. And now a dash of this—so. Now taste and see if you like.'

They tasted and said it was delicious, and after a short time spent in listening to their hostess's view on local wines, rose to take their leave.

'You must tell me,' said the Baronesa, 'where you are staying. I shall send your suitcases.'

'We're at a place called the Pensão Pombal,' said Mr. Channing.

There was a pause. The Baronesa's eyes, resting enquiringly on him, seemed to widen.

'I did not quite hear,' she said at last. 'The...'

'Not too good at the local pronunciation, I'm afraid,' said Mr. Channing. 'Pen-sow Pom-barl.'

'The ... the Pensão Pombal?' repeated the Baronesa faintly.

'That's the place.'

'But'—she looked from him to his wife, her hands outspreads—'but this place, this Pensão, is ...' She closed her eyes and shuddered and then stared at them incredulously. 'It is not a place for people such as ourselves.'

'They're clean, and very kind,' said Mrs. Channing.

'Clean! Kind! But ...' The Baronesa's voice grew in strength and conviction. 'But it is monstrous! Your friend put you there?'

'Well, yes. You see—' began Mr. Channing.

'But it is for peasants! It is where my servants place their friends when they come here to Sintra to visit. It is little better than a *taverna*, a ... You shall not stay there!'

'It's a pretty little place. In any case, we understood,' said Mr. Channing, 'that most other places were full.'

'Full? Perhaps the hotels, the *pensoes* are full. But here in my house,' declared the Baronesa passionately, 'there is room. There are rooms for my friends and you shall use them. Never'—she held up a large, beringed hand, stopping the protests of Mr. Channing and his wife—'never shall anybody say that I, Cielle, Baronesa Narvão, allowed my friends to remain in such a place. In the name of my adopted country, Portugal, I ask you to forgive that you should have been placed somewhere which is not suitable for you. From today, from this moment, you shall be here with me. Arturo'—he appeared and stood before her—'will see about it. You shall be shown at once to your rooms, and your luggage will be sent for, and you will give me the pleasure to have you here with me.'

'But—' began Mr. Channing.

'No refusal, I beg!' entreated the Baronesa.

'We really—' began Mrs. Channing.

She could say no more. The Baronesa had taken her hands and was speaking in a tone of appeal.

'You shall persuade your husband,' she said. 'I beg that you will not deprive me of such pleasure. Say to him that you will be my guest.'

Mrs. Channing hesitated. She herself wanted very much to stay at the Pensão Pombal; she liked Gustavo and his family and she realized, moreover, that as tourists, they had been peculiarly fortunate to have the opportunity of seeing something of Portuguese family life. But she was unable, for once, to guess her husband's wishes. He admired the

93

Baronesa; she could not remember when she had seen him come so far out of his anti-social shell. This was a beautiful house and, more important, a beautiful garden. If he would be happier here than at the Pensão Pombal...

'You're ... you're very kind,' she said. 'Perhaps—'

It was consent enough for the Baronesa. In an instant she was issuing orders to a succession of servants, demonstrating the international character of the establishment by changing effortlessly from Portuguese to French or German as the occasion required. She set the household into swift motion, and the Channings might as effectively have tried to dam a river as halt her in her hospitable preparations. They were taken upstairs to a room that looked like a bridal suite, and Christine was accommodated in a smaller room opposite. Flowers were brought in in vases, towels were placed in their bathrooms, pink-uniformed maids with starched white collars and cuffs and lacy aprons followed a severe-looking, black-clad woman and did her bidding.

When they went downstairs, Mrs. Channing told the Baronesa that she felt it necessary to go herself to the Pensão Pombal rather than remain here while their luggage was sent for. She would like to say good-bye, and her husband must pay their bill.

'Very well; since this is how you feel, then

94

you shall go,' the Baronesa said. 'But you will come back and be my guests. I shall send you in the car, and it will wait for you. Do not let them argue with you; my chauffeur will tell them that it is useless. And do not forget to get from them your passports, if you have given them up. Did they take them?'

'No.'

'They should have asked you at once. It is the law, even if people stay only for a short time.'

Mr. and Mrs. Channing were driven to the Pensão Pombal, and on the way there, Mrs. Channing learned that her husband would have preferred to stay on instead of moving to the Baronesa's house.

'It was hard to refuse,' he acknowledged. 'If she hadn't been standing between us, I could perhaps have sent you some kind of signal.'

'I thought you'd enjoy that garden.'

'Well, perhaps I shall. We can't stay there long; we shall have to look round for another place.'

They arrived at the Pensão Pombal, and after one glance at the Baronesa's car, Josefina seemed to lose all her smiles and her gaiety. The change of plan was explained to a silent, sober Gustavo. Mrs. Channing went upstairs, followed by Maria-Jose, Maria-Helena and Maria-Innocencia, and did the packing. The cases were carried out and placed in the car and they were driven back to the Quinta Narvão.

Mr. Channing gave the three passports into the Baronesa's keeping and followed her out on to the terrace and, looking at the lawns and the flower-beds, wondered how many gardeners were needed to keep a place like this in this kind of order.

Dinner, the Baronesa told them, would be at eight-thirty; what she spoke of as the preparation gong would sound at a quarter to eight. From this the Channings understood that they were expected to change, and when they met the Baronesa in the drawing-room before dinner, Mr. Channing was in a dinner-jacket only a little strained across the chest, Mrs. Channing was wearing a dress long known in the family as My Black, and Christine had reluctantly put on the dress she had worn as bridesmaid at her brother's wedding. The Baronesa herself, regal in a gown of shimmering green, confirmed Mr. Channing's impression that she must, when younger, have been a remarkably good-looking woman.

The drawing-room was white and gold, the dining-room red and gold. The food, served by three white-gloved menservants, was of superlative standard; Christine ate with frank enjoyment, Mrs. Channing tried to guess how each dish had been made, while Mr. Channing, unprepared for so many courses, ate too much fish and was unable to enjoy the tender, juicy steak that came next-but-one.

Drinking coffee in the drawing-room after dinner, there was time to note the beauty of the furniture, the richness of the curtains, the exquisite colours of the almost priceless rugs. The glass-fronted cabinets, standing here and there about the room, were filled with a variety of china and jade figures, as well as ornaments of gold and silver. The Baronesa seemed to want nothing more than to share with her guests her own frank pleasure in her possessions.

'You, I am quite sure, love your home,' she said to Mrs. Channing. 'I too love mine. Everything in it I love. Wherever my eyes look, I see beauty, and this pleases me. When the king—please excuse me if I do not say which; this embarrasses, isn't it?—stayed here with me, he said again and again: Dear Cielle, here only I feel at home; here only I see taste without fault, choice without error. He gave me that beautiful set of china you see over there. Take it, Cielle, he begged me; take it and make it feel at home—for where, poor man, could he now keep anything?' She saw Christine's eyes on the bracelet she was wearing, and held up her ample but shapely arm. 'You are looking at my little bracelet? The princess gave it to me; I cannot, forgive me, say which. How she loved me, that dear woman! She had worn the bracelet since her wedding day; other things were on it then, little golden hearts, for many men had loved her. But those, of course, I refused to take.'

They looked at the delicate gold band; it looked at first glance like a charm bracelet, but they saw that instead of charms, a dozen tiny gold keys hung from it.

'Do the keys open anything?' Mrs. Channing asked.

'Ah, but yes! That is why I had them made. They are of course gold. My husband said to me: Cielle, you have beautiful things; you must guard them. And so I do. Here on my wrist, always, are the keys to my cabinets. Only when I take my bath each morning do I take them off, and then immediately, I put them on again.' She rose, selected a key and, holding her arm close to one of the cabinets, opened it. 'Come and see,' she invited.

They went closer. The Baronesa lifted gently, one by one, the little carved jade figures that stood on the shelves.

'Nobody in the world, I think,' she said, 'has these. One piece, two, perhaps four or six—but a whole set, no. I cannot tell you, but of course you can see, what fabulous value these have. The queen—you must forgive me if I do not say which queen—gave me the first of my collection. After her, the prince, her son. When he married, he said to me: Cielle, but for you I should not have met my wife—and for gratitude, he gave me the rest of the collection. One piece alone is worth having, for such work is rare. To have a whole set is perhaps a great risk. Certainly it is a trouble, for now the princess and her relations, who have no right to any of this, pester me and say that I should return them to the family. That is nonsense, of course.' She replaced the figures carefully, locked the case and jingled the bracelet complacently. 'Always,' she told them, 'I remember what my husband said to me: Collect. Collect, Cielle, collect, he said. Jewels, treasures—and this I have done. My friends have been kind, and what they gave me, I keep.'

She opened the next cabinet, and the next. At last she led the Channings, somewhat bemused by kings and princes and treasure, for a cooling walk on the terrace. A servant wheeled out a little wagon on which were decanters and glasses, ice, frosted jugs filled with fruit drinks and a variety of sandwiches for those whom five courses had failed to fill. Having said good night to their hostess, they were escorted to their rooms and left to cool, faintly-scented linen sheets.

For the next two days, they were offered the same perfection of service—and admitted to one another that it was wasted on them. Luxury at this level seemed to Mrs. Channing out of gear with the times. Mr. Channing longed for simpler living and plainer fare, and confided to his wife that a little of the Baronesa went a very long way. Christine dismissed the whole thing as pure musical comedy; watching the Baronesa sweeping in to dinner, she expected the maids to perform the Can-Can and the menservants to provide a rousing male chorus. She had no wish, she said, to spoil her parents' enjoyment, if any, but she would like to move back to the verandah with the tin tables, and the sooner the better.

It was soon enough. On the fifth morning everything, as she was to tell James later, blew up right in their faces.

CHAPTER FIVE

On the evening of the second day of their visit, Mr. Channing, after consultation with his wife, decided that he would speak to the Baronesa in the morning and tell her that they must leave. But he found that there was no opportunity, the next day or the day following, to raise the question of departure; the Baronesa had arranged a programme of sight-seeing for them, and they spent the two days driving to churches and museums, walking round palaces and gardens and visit night clubs to hear *fados*. As all the meals on these expeditions were taken in restaurants, Mr. Channing found them expensive; he felt that it was out of the question to allow the Baronesa, after all her kindness, to be put to extra expense, and so was obliged to pay the bills himself. Counting his rapidly-dwindling supply of money, he realized that spending at this level could not continue. It was decided that on the following morning he would inform the Baronesa, with regret and gratitude, of their decision to leave.

'You must be firm,' Mrs. Channing said. 'Don't let her talk you into changing your mind.'

'If he adds up what he's spent in the past two days,' said Christine, 'he'll be as firm as a rock. Tell her I'm tired of being formal. If I'd thought that marrying James meant living like this, I couldn't have faced it, but I'm glad to say we can cut out all the pomp. If I could have got into my pants and put my feet on the sofa I could have stood it better, but all this king-I-won't-say-which is, frankly, wearing me down.'

'I'll speak to the Baronesa,' said Mr. Channing.

The Baronesa did not come down to breakfast. Having finished his own, Mr. Channing looked for her and found her at last in the Chinese room, a small apartment opposite the drawing-room containing jade and lacquer enough to justify its name, but whose chief article of furniture was a large desk which, seeing it open for the first time, surprised Mr. Channing by its row of business-like pigeon holes, each filled with neat piles of papers. The Baronesa herself, seated at the desk, turned at his entrance and gave him a cordial greeting. Rising, pen in hand, she waved him to a chair.

'Good morning, good morning! How is it that your wife is not with you on this beautiful day? She did not sleep badly? Sit down, sit down.'

'No, thank you, I won't stay more than a moment; I can see you're busy. I just wanted to catch you and—'

'Ah! That is not easy, today. I have so much, so much, so much, too much, to do! Here'—she indicated the papers on the desk—'here are the things that I have been neglecting because I wanted to show you some pretty places. It is so dull for you, who do not know Portugal, to go about by yourselves, with nobody to guide, nobody to explain. So many people go to the wrong places, look at the wrong things, isn't it?'

'Well, yes. I suppose—'

'But today you must forgive me. Today I must be chained here, in this room, at my desk. I have fallen into—how do you put it?—into arrears. I must catch it up. There is so much to do, and I have nobody who helps me in this way.' She sighed. 'But business is business, no?'

Mr. Channing, without premonitions of any kind, agreed. Business, however distasteful, was still business.

'And so,' went on the Baronesa, 'I have drawn up your account. There will of course be more, but the most is here. If there is anything I have escaped, I know that you will point this out.'

Her words, reaching Mr. Channing as they did without the slightest warning or preparation, did not at first seem to have any meaning. But if his mind lagged behind, his eyes, falling to the long sheet of paper the Baronesa handed him, opened instantly to the terrible truth.

The sheet was headed Quinta de Narvão. Under the heading was printed, on the left hand side, a full and complete list of hotel charges. Not one corresponding line on the opposite side had been left unfilled. The total, when Mr. Channing's eyes rested on it, gave him for a moment a dreadful sense of giddiness; a loud buzzing sounded in his ears.

Something in him fought for self-control. He must pull himself together, and before too many moments had gone by. He must say something. He could not stand here indefinitely, staring at the account in his hand.

He raised his eyes to hers, and her expression, at once bold and bland, wary and expectant, told him that this was a situation she had faced many times before. He was too confused to think; he spoke the first words that came to his tongue.

'You'll think me incredibly stupid,' he said, 'but I must say at once that I had no idea ... I made the mistake of thinking that your kind offer was ...' He cleared his throat. 'I did not realize,' he said more firmly, 'that your house was ... that...'

'Are you trying to tell me'—her tone, belying the expression in her eyes, was incredulous—'that you did not know that I had to make some little charges?' She raised her shoulders in a long-sustained shrug. 'But my dear Mr. Channing, did you, could you suppose that ... After all, one could not say that we were old friends. Isn't it?'

'I should,' he repeated, 'have realized what the situation was. But to be frank, I didn't.'

Her eyebrows went up; her expression became one of open contempt.

'But come, Mr. Channing! Does one make these offers to strangers? Do strangers—I have no wish to hurt your feelings, but you are at this rate hurting mine—do strangers accept hospitality of this nature, on such a scale, after such brief acquaintance?'

'No. No, they don't. I should have—'

'You are, after all, a man of the world. How could you suppose that I would lavish—I hope you will allow me to say lavish, because this is true of the hospitality I give—could you suppose that I would do this after speaking once, twice, to a gentleman on a steamer? Me, the Baronesa Narvão? Am I so friendless, so much without resource, that I should ... No! This you could not have imagined! I am not, after all, anybody. Even if through misfortune I am obliged to turn my house into an hotel, I

104

am still who I am. I am sorry, my dear Mr. Channing, but you cannot make me believe such a thing. You cannot offer me this insult.'

There was a short silence, but Mr. Channing's head was now clear. The shock, great as it was, had been absorbed. He knew where he was—and with humiliation more bitter than he had ever experienced, he knew what he was. He was a dupe—an easy victim. She had seen him, had sized him up without difficulty. She had recognized him for the bumpkin, the clodhopper that he was. He had shown himself, from first to last, a fool of the first order.

He had looked too long, he told himself bitterly, at his flowers. While he had been in his garden, the world had gone by. He had left the business of life to his wife. She had brought up his children, ordered his household and fought his battles. He had emerged at last from his long retreat, and had learned exactly how he appeared to the world: a gullible fool.

He let his glance, clear and cold, rest once more upon the bill.

'I see,' he said quietly, 'that you have charged us for the meals of the past two days. Perhaps you forget that—'

'If you are going to say that we had these meals elsewhere, I would rather'—she made a gesture of distaste—'I would rather not hear this. Can I cancel the order for lunch, for dinner, when at any moment it might begin to rain, when you or your wife or your daughter may change their minds and say: No, we shall not go out? This, as you must now know, is an hotel, and in hotels, must there not always be meals if wished for? Have you,' she demanded, 'any complaints to make about the quality of my hospitality?'

'None,' he replied with dignity. 'My only complaint, Baronesa, is against myself for my stupidity.'

'Stupidity,' she said incredibly, 'must always be paid for.'

He stared at her, speechless, and saw in her glance open and undisguised boredom, and contempt. She closed the desk, locked it and walked past him to the door.

'One moment,' he said.

She turned to face him.

'Well? What now?'

'This account is for a month. My wife and daughter and I decided this morning that—kind as we believed you to be—we could not trespass any longer on your hospitality. I came in here to tell you that we were leaving tomorrow.'

'Can you,' she said in amazed enquiry, 'expect me to believe such a thing? When I asked you on the ship how long you would stay, what did you answer? A month. And now you say, after only these few days, no more. For you, how many people have I not sent away? How many have I refused, even when they begged? I told them that for a month, my house was full. I may be an hotel, but I take three guests only; to take more would make it less perfect, less private, less intimate. What your plans are, to be made and to be unmade, is not my concern; you said a month and you must pay a month. This is only justice. If you have not brought enough money with you— and this is something that English people nearly always do, for some reason I do not have time to understand—then please to give me a cheque on your English bank. This will be quite all right; I have ways to cash it.'

She went out, leaving the door open. He was alone ... with the bill in his hand. He had to go upstairs and face his wife, face Christine and tell them that he—husband, father, protector, provider, support—had been the easy victim of a stale confidence trick. While he had bowed and babbled his gratitude, the Baronesa had sat at the desk drawing up the bill. He had been swindled, and that was hard enough to bear, but to be swindled in this way, to have his self-respect stripped brutally from him, to be labelled a cadger who hastened to accept hospitality on this scale from a woman, a widow of title, who had thrown a few words at him on the deck of a liner—this was a punishment that nothing in his past life seemed to merit.

When at last he brought himself to go upstairs, he found his rooms empty. From one of the windows he saw his wife and daughter seated on one of the white-painted, cushioned iron benches in the garden. He went down and walked across the lawn to join them.

Mrs. Channing, glancing at her husband's face, felt her heart turning within her. Beyond getting up and going a step or two to meet him, she gave no sign. Christine, her expression unreadable, made room for him on the bench.

'I won't sit down,' he said. 'What I have to say can best be said standing up. Or perhaps there's no need to say anything.' He held out the bill. 'You'd both better look at that.'

Mrs. Channing took it, and Christine got up and looked over her shoulder. After an interval during which nobody said anything, Mrs. Channing folded the paper and handed it back to her husband.

'Sit down,' she said quietly.

He sat down and stared unseeingly at a carpet of varied, beautiful flowers.

'It's rather hard to bear,' he said at last, and both his wife and his daughter were aware that in this trouble, money values had little or no part. Mrs. Channing clenched her hands tightly in her lap, and Christine, driven to action, made a savage lunge at a wasp buzzing nearby. Then she swung round and started at her father.

'All you did,' she said, 'was what anybody else would have done. She's a cheat, and we're not used to cheats and so we didn't spot her, that's all.'

'She called me, with the greatest contempt,' Mr. Channing brought out slowly, 'a man of the world. As a man of the world—she said—I must have known that her invitation was not given out of friendship. She was right.'

'She's a dirty, low-down, swindling harpy,' Christine said fiercely. 'Are you going to sit there and tell us that just because you didn't smell her out from the start, you're to blame? Can't you see she does this all the time? I *felt* she was phony. I felt all the time that she—'

'But I didn't,' her father said.

The quiet words silenced her. Tears of rage and pity came into her eyes and she fought them back. Cry? For that big horse of a smooth-tongued cheat? Never.

'Tell him,' she said abruptly to her mother.

'In a moment,' Mrs. Channing said.

Her husband turned to look at her.

'Tell me what?'

'Nothing. Just sit quiet for a little while.'

'I'll tell you,' said Christine. 'That bill may have been a nasty surprise to you, but it wasn't such a shock to Mother and to me.'

'You mean'—her father looked up at her—'that you and your mother had already—'

'We didn't know there'd be a bill, but we were sitting here waiting for something to happen. Because on our way out of the house, we looked for you because Mother wanted to remind you to ask for our passports. We met the Baronesa, so we asked her for them.'

'She said'—Mrs. Channing took up the story—'that she had mislaid them. They were in a drawer to which she had lost the key. I asked if it would be possible, in the event of her not finding it, to have another key made.'

'What did she say?'

'Nothing. She smiled in a peculiar way and just walked past us. Christine and I didn't know what to make of it, but I remembered that when we came here, she had made a point of reminding you about our passports—and she took them from us the moment we entered the house. It didn't seem possible that anything could be wrong, but it does look as though she won't give the passports back until this bill is paid.'

There was a long silence. At the end of it, Mr. Channing got to his feet.

'I'm going in,' he said, 'to write her a cheque. She said she could cash a cheque on my English bank.'

'But'—Christine put both hands on his coat sleeve and held him—'but that bill's for a month's stay! It's one thing to pay for what we've had, but it's quite another thing to sit down under sheer daylight robbery!'

'We won't see those passports again,' Mr. Channing said, 'until I've paid her in full. There has been humiliation enough. All I can do now is pay her—and get away.'

'But—' began Christine.

'I would like,' Mrs. Channing said suddenly, 'to get outside. Outside that gate. Just for a little while.'

They turned and looked at her white face.

'Madeleine, I'm sorry,' Mr. Channing said. 'You don't ... you don't know how I feel.'

She looked up at him.

'You feel a fool,' she said quietly. 'We've been made fools of. We needn't feel too bad; we haven't done anything worse than allow ourselves to believe an experienced liar. But I must get away—out of her house—for an hour or two. Couldn't we ... couldn't we go for a walk or something?'

They went out on to the road and walked slowly down the hill towards the town centre, and presently Mr. Channing voiced the thought that was in all their minds.

'Perhaps,' he said, 'this is why the Colonel—'

He paused.

'I bet he knew,' said Christine.

Since leaving the Pensão Pombal they had twice called at the Colonel's house, and finding him and his wife out, had left a note asking him to get in touch with them at the Quinta de Narvão. No message had been received, and Mr. Channing had begun to wonder if the Colonel resented their leaving so precipitately the accommodation he had chosen for them. Now another reason for the Colonel's silence had become apparent.

111

They sat at a table outside a café opposite the Palace and ordered coffee, and after a glance at the pale faces of her parents, Christine attempted some form of consolation.

'Look, let's see this straight,' she said. 'We've been done. We've been skinned; we've been plucked and cooked. But it wasn't because she saw straw sticking out of our hair. She's bound to have a different approach for every kind of—'

She stopped. A voice from across the way had called her name in loud and joyous accents. She looked round, looked up and saw in the large courtyard of the Palace a young man gesticulating in the hope of attracting her attention. He came hurrying across the road, his face alight with pleasure and excitement, and seized her hands. He was tall, rather loose-jointed, with a long, thin face more amiable than intellectual.

'Christine! How absolutely marvellous!' he exclaimed. 'What are you doing here?'

'What,' she asked, 'brought *you* to Sintra?'

'Duty.' He glanced expectantly at Christine's parents, and she performed an introduction.

'My mother and father. This is Charles Granger.'

'An enormous pleasure,' said Charles, with obvious sincerity. 'Any parent of Christine's is ... I mean, I've been looking forward to ...'

'Won't you join us?' Mrs. Channing asked,

trying to remember where she had heard his name.

'I'd love to. Thanks very much. Would you excuse me a moment while I just go across and tell my aunt I'm leaving her?'

'Oh, but—' Mrs. Channing protested.

'I was going round the Palace with her. We'd have been inside by now if she hadn't met a couple of old friends on the steps. Back in a minute.'

'I've heard the name,' Mrs. Channing said, as he went away. 'But...'

'He was the one who directed James to the Battersea Dogs' Home,' said Christine.

Mr. Channing looking bewildered.

'James wanted a dog?'

'No. James wanted me.'

Charles came back, pulled out a chair, said, in answer to Mr. Channing's enquiry, that he would have a beer, and went on talking.

'Couldn't believe it,' he told Christine. 'I looked across the road and there you were. Illusion, I said to myself. Blinked once or twice and looked again—same girl, same place. Haven't seen you for months. You went into hiding with James, and people were beginning to think there was something in it, but I scanned *The Times* and didn't see anything. Are you in or out of circulation?'

'Out,' said Christine, after consideration.

'Then why aren't you blinding us all with a finger-full of diamonds? Are you engaged or disengaged?'

'Drink your beer,' said Christine. 'What duty do you have towards your aunt?'

'Well, confidentially'—he glanced apologetically at Mr. and Mrs. Channing—'she's supposed to be leaving me her all—one day. My parents insist on my coming out here every year, which is really a great waste. I mean to say, I like the old ... I'm quite fond of my aunt, but a change is a change. She pays my fare out and back, of course, but I've never been able to induce her to pay it in cash so that I could use it to go somewhere else. I've nothing against the old ... I mean, I wouldn't say this to everyone, but as we're all old friends I don't mind telling you that she's just a little'—he held his thumb and forefinger a quarter of an inch apart—'just a *leetle* demented. Quite harmless, naturally, or she wouldn't be around, even with me. She's just got this idea that she once lived in the Palace as the rightful owner—not this time round, I don't mean, but in a previous incarceration, or do I mean incantation? Anyhow, apart from this little peculiarity, she's fairly sane, on the whole. She travels a good deal—in fact, she's almost always on the trot, and to the most incredible places; the only time you can really pin her down is now—she spends the summer in Portugal. I wouldn't mind doing this yearly duty if it could be varied a bit, but it's always Sintra, Sintra, Sintra. Incidentally, where are you staying?'

There was a pause.

'We started off,' Christine said, 'at a little place called the Pensão Pombal.'

'Never heard of it. In Sintra?'

'Yes. As a matter of fact, we'd like to move. Does your aunt have any influence?'

'I could ask her. She's not too keen on dishing out advice of this kind, because some friends of hers came out in the spring and she'd fixed them up at some hotel or other and went to the airport to tell them so, when they informed her they didn't want the rooms; they'd met a charming lady in the airport lounge who'd invited them to stay with her. Well, the so-called lady turned out to be a shark of the first water—I'm not trying to be funny, by the way—who's well known round these parts, but who goes on catching new fish all the time. My aunt tried to put in a word of warning, but they thought she was annoyed at having been put to trouble for nothing. A few days later they were on her doorstep screeching that they'd been taken in, in both senses of the term. It's a sort of hobby here, looking to see who the Baronesa—this old shark's a Baronesa—has got hold of. Sort of local joke. Her line is asking people to stay on a friendly basis and then presenting a staggering bill. You wouldn't think there were so many people in the world simply asking to be eaten by sharks, but there it is: one born every minute, they say.

115

Look here, you've finished your coffee. May I order you something else?'

'No, you can't,' Christine said. 'You can go on telling us about the people who love being eaten. Not the last lot. We know about the last lot. We were the last lot.'

'Oh, people are always being...'

Charles stopped abruptly as the meaning of her words went home. Open-mouthed, he stared from one member of the family to the other.

'I ... I ... You ... You mean you...'

'Yes,' said Christine.

'Good God! How ... I mean where...'

'She came out on the same boat as we did and offered to take some of our luggage. When we went to collect it, she invited us, begged us to stay with her. The bill was presented this morning. And now, if you don't mind, we'll talk about something else.'

But Mr. Channing was not ready to change the conversation.

'Do I understand,' he asked, 'that this woman is well known in Sintra?'

'And in Lisbon too,' answered Charles. 'She's what's known as a by-word. If she tried any of this locally, she'd run up against people who know all about her—but she doesn't operate locally. She finds an unceasing supply of suckers and ... I mean,' he ended lamely, 'she doesn't fish in home waters.'

Mr. Channing rose.

'If that's the case,' he said, 'I'll go round and have a word with a friend of mine. Do you know Colonel Bell-Burton?'

'My aunt talks about him, and I've seen him around,' said Charles, 'but I—'

'I think your mother and I,' Mr. Channing told Christine, 'will go and see if he's at home. If he isn't, I shall write a note and leave it for him. He might be able to give me some advice.'

'If you've got into the old Baronesa's clutches, sir,' Charles told him frankly, 'it isn't advice you need; it's a money-lender.'

'While you're at the Colonel's,' Christine said, 'couldn't I go round to the Pombal and see if they've still got our rooms? If they have, couldn't we go back there? I don't want to spend another night under that harpy's roof.'

Her father looked at her, his face for the first time in the past hour showing a gleam of hope. He was remembering their welcome at the Pombal, and the warm handshakes and homely atmosphere and he longed, with an intensity that shook him, to be back there again.

'That wouldn't,' he said, 'be at all a bad idea. Your mother and I will meet you here in an hour.'

Colonel Bell-Burton was at home, but his manner had something of restraint.

'Come in, come in,' he said. 'I'm sorry Thelma isn't here; she likes to go out with the children and keep an eye on the Nanny, who isn't at all the kind we would have chosen—but it's nothing to do with us, of course. Come along in.'

He led the visitors into a large, square drawing-room, and at any other time the view from its windows would have drawn exclamations of pleasure from Mr. and Mrs. Channing—but they were not thinking of views.

'Sit down,' the Colonel said. 'I ...' He hesitated. 'You moved out of the Pombal, I see. Wasn't much of a place, of course; felt bad putting you there, but Thelma said it was clean and—'

'We liked it,' Mrs. Channing said. 'We would have stayed there, but—'

'We may as well be frank,' her husband broke in. 'We've just heard that being done down by the Baronesa Narvão is a local joke. Well, we're not laughing. I got the bill this morning—for a month's stay. I'm not blaming anybody but myself. A man of my age ought to do better, know better than—'

'Now stop that,' said the Colonel firmly. 'I'll be frank too. When I heard you were there, I ... well, my heart sank. I felt I ought to go straight up there and get you all out. But what would you have said if I had? If you'd believed me, what could you have done? You would have got your month's bill just the same. You've nothing to reproach yourself for. She's an old hand. She's too clever at it to—'

'But I don't understand,' Mrs. Channing said. 'Does she do this all the time?'

'Year in and year out. You see,' the Colonel explained, 'her strong suit is that—speaking purely of externals—she's genuine enough. Her title's genuine, her house is splendid, the gardens—we all get in once a year on payment of a stiff entrance fee—well worth looking at. She's got a well-trained staff and a magnificent chef. So you see that from her point of view, it's her value for your money.'

'But she could advertise and get guests who'd know what they were paying,' Mrs. Channing pointed out. 'Why trap people like us?'

'You'd be surprised,' the Colonel said, 'how few people want, or will pay for her brand of palatial hospitality. Who, coming to a place like Sintra, wants that Arabian Nights setup? Who, with that kind of money—to put it another way—wants to stay in a semi-private establishment when they can use a five-star hotel and enjoy its amenities without having to have the Baronesa too? And while Sintra's pleasant enough, it doesn't attract year-round, millionaire visitors. If she came into the open, she might do well enough for the two or three crowded months, but she'd be empty most of the rest of the year—and as she can't afford to live without guests, she'd have to reduce her standard. But she won't. She likes living in that way, in that style; as she can't pay for it, someone else has to. Her husband left her the house, but no money to keep it up. Her expenses are enormous, therefore her charges have to be enormous.'

'How long has she been doing this?' Mr. Channing asked.

'Certainly as long as I've been here, which is over sixteen years. As far as I know, those rooms of hers have never been empty for more than a few days, winter or summer. She keeps a look-out on the quays and on the tarmac and you'd be surprised how often she lands people whose other arrangements, for some reason or another, have fallen through. Did you know she brought out a couple of Great Danes?'

'Yes. I saw her exercising them,' Mr. Channing said. 'She told me she was doing it for a friend.'

'If he was a friend before, he isn't a friend now. He's an Englishman who came out to settle here, and bought a rather nice house on the hills between here and Lisbon. The Baronesa heard he'd bought a couple of Great Danes and was looking for someone who'd keep an eye on them on the journey out from England. The Baronesa said she would—and as you see, she did. She mentioned, casually and I've no doubt charmingly to this fellow that of course he might meet her in the matter of expenses, and like a fool he wrote off to her in England to say she must of course charge him for her out-of-pocket expenses. The place

120

was buzzing yesterday with the news that she'd charged him her entire trip there and back—and the wording of his letter was ambiguous enough to land him in trouble if he refused payment. I tell you this to prove that she's too clever for people with twice your toughness. It goes without saying, of course, that she's got your passports?'

'Yes.'

'That's part of the routine—the most important part, of course. You won't see them again, I'm afraid, until she sees her money. I don't want to depress you, but I've never once heard of anyone who got away without paying in full—and in cash.'

'She said she'd take a cheque on my English bank,' said Mr. Channing.

'What she didn't say,' replied the Colonel, 'was that you wouldn't see your passports until she'd cashed it. If you want money, I'll let you have it. You can give me a cheque, and with the cash to give her, you can get out as soon as you want to.'

'That's very kind of you. If you'd really not mind—'

'Pleasure. I'll go along to the bank with you when you leave.'

'Doesn't she ever pick on anybody who can't pay?' Mrs. Channing asked. 'After all, we're not rich.'

'You could afford to pay first-class fares for a holiday. Considered as a hotel bill, the sum is

121

outrageous, but it isn't, after all, a larger sum than people like you can pay. What she banks on, why she chooses people like you, is the fact that you'll fight her up to a certain point—but after that, rather than get involved in real unpleasantness, you chuck in your hand and pay up and get out. The idea of making you pay for a long stay is, of course, to give her time to look for the next lot of—'

He stopped, and Mr. Channing supplied the words grimly.

'—naïve fools.'

'Don't blame yourself too much,' the Colonel advised. 'She's an old hand at this. What makes me sick is that if I hadn't been so tied up with other things when you arrived, I could have kept you out of trouble. I saw her there on the quay; I realized she'd travelled out with you—but with you all safe, as I thought, at the Pombal, how could I dream she'd get her claws into you?—Where's Christine, by the way?'

'She's gone to the Pombal to see if they've still got our rooms. If they have, I'll go back there. I'm not going—in spite of that bill—to go straight back home with my tail between my legs. We'll see what the Pombal has to offer.'

Christine had not lingered at the café.

'I'm going to see about those rooms,' she said to Charles. 'Want to come?'

He gave an eager assent, and then sent a hunted look across the road.

'I ought to hang around here,' he said. 'My aunt...'

'I thought you said she'd met some friends.'

'She'll go round the Palace with them, but I ought to be there to take charge when she comes out. Left on her own, she's apt to start something. You may think that keeping an eye on an old girl is easy, but with my aunt it isn't all oranges and lemons, I can tell you.'

'Well, I'll leave you to her,' Christine said. 'See you some time.'

'Wait a minute.' He put out a hand to detain her. 'I wanted to say something. Is it true that you're not engaged?'

'If you mean am I free to resume the tepid affair we were having, the answer's no.'

'Tepid?' Charles sounded indignant. 'It might have been tepid on your side, but I was jolly serious, I can tell you!'

'What were you serious about?'

'About marrying you, of course. It didn't come up as a definite proposition, but while my old aunt's still on her feet and padding round the castle, what do I have to offer?'

'What became of that girl called Joan something?'

'Joanna? She went to Bermuda on a cruise, and stayed there. You don't think there was anything in that, do you?'

'Weren't you engaged for a time to Brenda Pont?'

'That was a mistake anybody could have

123

made. I got two days hunting a week because she lent me her father's horses. I thanked her a bit too warmly, and there you are. She broke it off to go show-jumping. Instead of running down my list, why don't you explain all those months you spent choking everybody but James off?'

'I'm going to marry him.'

'Marry ... But you said—'

'I said I wasn't engaged. Well, I'm not. We decided to wait three months.'

'Wait what for?'

'To see if it sticks.'

'To see ... Hasn't anybody ever told James about the dangers of over-confidence? Or you, for that matter?'

Christine, on the point of telling him that the three months had not been her idea, or James's, decided against it. Charles had some good points, but discretion wasn't one of them.

'It gives James a chance to pick up a millionairess,' she said.

'It's a stinking idea,' Charles said frankly, 'and if he wanted to pick up a millionairess, that cousin of his was around, wasn't she? I always understood she was being iced ready for his next birthday, and that's one reason I tried to put him off the scent when he angled for an introduction to you. He had a girl—I thought—and one's enough for any man. One at a time, I mean. I never met this cousin, but they tell me she's worth three million. I might have a go myself while she's here.'

For a moment, Christine was too surprised to speak.

'Here? *Here?*' she brought out at last.

Charles was almost as surprised as she was.

'You mean James didn't tell you?'

'He ...' She decided against revealing the fact that she and James were not in communication with one another. 'No, he didn't. D'you mean she's here in Sintra?'

'Just out of. She and her mother are staying with that French family who've just bought the Quinta dos Castanheiros—that's that spread you can see on that hill over there. You can't see the house for the chestnuts, but you get a glimpse of a couple of white towers sticking up. My aunt says the mother breeds dogs; the millions, I gather, belong to her daughter and not to her. I don't know why James didn't tell you to look them up; they're here, I gather, for about three weeks.'

Christine did not answer. Surprise had given place to a relief so great that she had to struggle against an unwise impulse to throw her arms round Charles and embrace him. Katherine— Katherine Staples—wasn't in England. She wasn't near James. She was here, miles away from James, the wide sea between them.

It had been all very well, she realized, as she gazed round at a scene that had in the past few minutes assumed a charm she had hitherto missed, it had been all very well to remind

125

herself that James had had years in which to fall in love with his cousin. They had met frequently, both in the north and in London; if he'd wanted her, there she was, free and unattached. The thought had been reassuring up to a point, but there had been obvious danger in his being subjected to three months of persuasion, with Katherine Staples thrown at him at every turn.

But Katherine Staples was here, among the chestnut trees, with her mother who bred dogs, and James was at home in Northumberland, and life was wonderful.

She remembered that Charles was still standing beside her.

'Are you coming with me, or not?' she asked him.

'I'd like to—but my aunt ... Perhaps I could—'

'No; I'll go by myself. You go back to her and—' She broke off, her eyes, wide and incredulous, fixed on something over Charles's shoulder. 'Is that ... is that her?' she enquired, too awed to think of the nicer points of grammar.

An elderly woman—tall, thin to the point of emaciation—was coming down the steps of the Palace. She was dressed in the tight trousers and loose sweater currently in favour with teenagers; her feet were thrust into scarlet sandals. Under fashionably tousled blue-white hair, Christine saw a raddled, painted, shrewd

126

old face.

'That's her,' said Charles. 'What's more, she's seen me.'

His aunt was coming across the road, calling to him in a high, authoritative voice.

'Charles! Who's this pretty girl you've found?'

Charles, crimson with shame and embarrassment, mumbled an introduction, and his aunt, Lady Lovelle, took Christine's hand in hers.

'My dear, he's a genius!' she shrilled. 'Only out of my sight for five minutes, and look what he finds! Are you staying in Sintra?'

'We're unfortunately at the Quinta de Narvão,' Christine said, and saw Lady Lovelle's jaw drop. Releasing Christine's hand, she stood for a moment or two in an attitude of dismayed astonishment, and then spoke in a tone of wonder.

'How does she *do* it? Well, of course, one knows *how* she does it—by hunting round the quays and the airport and meeting the Sud Express and so on—but how is it that she always manages to get such charming people? She's a genius, like Charles. A crook, of course; that goes without saying. I suppose you've just got your bill?'

'My father got it this morning.'

'Well, tell him from me to pay without fuss; it's far, far better in the end. Pay—and leave.'

The first unfavourable impressions were

127

wearing off; in spite of Lady Lovelle's extraordinary appearance and parroquet voice, Christine was beginning to like her.

'That's what he means to do,' she said. 'I'm just going along to try and get the rooms we had before she persuaded us to go and stay with her.'

'Where were you before?'

'At the Pensão Pombal.'

'In Sintra?'

'Yes. Not far from here.'

'Well, I've never heard of it, but I'm sure it's very nice. Look, why don't you come and have lunch with me? I've got such nice people coming.'

'Oh Aunt Emily, you haven't asked a crowd again, have you?' Charles asked. 'Last time—'

'Quiet, Charles. Very nice people,' Lady Lovelle went on to Christine. 'Five altogether. I know two of them, and they know the others. I think it was five; it may have been six, but we shall know when they arrive. Do come!'

'I'm so sorry; I'm afraid I can't. It's very kind of you.'

'Well, some other time—if there *is* another time. Most people, after getting entangled with the Baronesa, make a bolt for home. Does she still sweep down to dinner in those backless gowns?'

'Yes.'

'I dare say she'll hold out until she gets too old, and then she'll have to sell off those gold

128

and jade and ivory collections. And her jewels, which they say are magnificent. You really have to give her credit, you know, for a sort of spirit of independence. Most women in her position and with her looks, would be looking for men, not for paying guests.'

'Look, Aunt Emily—'

'Quiet, Charles. Are you sure, Christine, that you can't come to lunch?'

'Quite sure, thank you.'

'Well, if you stay on here, you must meet me one day and let me take you over the Palace. I know it far better than those guides do. I lived there once; not in this existence, of course, but in another. I feel utterly at home there; I only wish I could remember who I was, but it's becoming a little clearer as I get older. I shall know one day. And now I'm afraid I shall have to take Charles away from you; I can't face all those people at lunch by myself. Come along, Charles.'

Christine went on her way pleased with the encounter, and shortly stopped to ask the way to the Pensão Pombal. Asking, she found, was easy; following the general direction of pointing fingers was also easy; what was more difficult was deciding, a few moments later, whether to go straight on, follow the left or right fork, or take a chance on the narrow lane that looked not unlike that leading to the Pombal but which might lead nowhere.

She located the Pensão at last, at the end of

the sixth lane. She halted at the edge of the courtyard and looked round at a scene that did not seem to have changed since she first saw it on her arrival with her parents. Only in Gustavo's face, as he came down the verandah steps and walked across to speak to her, was there a difference. The old friendliness was absent; he wore instead a wary and somewhat puzzled frown.

'Good morning,' said Christine.

He bowed. There was a pause during which Christine vowed to herself that her children, if any, would be taught twelve languages as well as their mother tongue; then she raised a finger and pointed to the house and in vivid mime gave Gustavo to understand that two rooms were required.

He nodded; obviously the rooms were free. Were there, he asked, holding up fingers in his turn, two people, or three?

Christine pointed to herself.

'For me,' she said. 'For me, for Senhor Papa, for Senhora Mama.'

'But ...' Gustavo pointed down the lane. 'Senhor, Senhora, Baronesa.'

'No.' Christine shook her head. 'Baronesa, no.' She made a gesture of putting something undesirable away from her. 'Baronesa adios. Senhor, Senhora, me ... *here*,' she ended firmly, pointing towards the house.

And that, she told herself, was the best she could do without further training. If she'd made it look as though the Baronesa had thrown them out, it was a pity, but it still meant that they needed the rooms.

With deep relief, she saw that light had broken over the face of Gustavo. She saw him turn away, and heard him give a roar—but this time it was not for his wife or his daughters; he called, instead, for Felipe.

The sound of wood-chopping ceased; from the rear of one of the outhouses came a stocky youth of about twenty-two dressed in jeans, a checked shirt and a black peaked cap. Gustavo seized him, dragged him towards Christine, exhibited him triumphantly and, hitting him hard on the chest, said:

'Eengleesh!'

The word was followed by a rapid open-and-shut movement of his hands to indicate the speed and fluency with which Felipe could speak.

'You speak English?' Christine asked him.

'Little. Unnerstand well,' Felipe said, giving her a wide, friendly smile. 'The lady tell me, I tell Gustavo.'

They walked together to the verandah, and on the way, Christine learned—not from Felipe but from Gustavo, who could not wait to have his statements translated, but whose gestures spoke more than words—that Felipe was engaged to Maria de Fatima; whenever his work brought him to Sintra during the day, he dropped into the Pensão hoping not only to see

131

her but to share whatever meal happened to be going. He was to stay for lunch, but it was only fair that he should earn it by doing some wood-chopping.

Gustavo placed Christine in a chair on the verandah, called for wine and set it before her. At her invitation, he and Felipe sat down; Felipe took off his cap and placed it carefully under his chair.

'Will you please tell Senhor Gustavo,' Christine asked him, 'that we are leaving the house of the Baronesa and we want to come back here.'

'She invite you?' Felipe enquired.

'Yes.'

'She say come as friend, and then give you big bill?'

'Yes.'

'She make you pay long time?'

'She charged us for a month.'

'You pay already? Finish?'

'No. My father is going to pay today, and then we want to come back here.'

'The Baronesa has taken your passports?'

'Yes.'

'Your father and mother—the Senhor and Senhora—are there still?'

'No. I'm going to meet them near the Palace in a little while. I came here to see if the rooms were still free.'

At this point, Christine saw that no more details were required of her. Felipe had turned

132

to Gustavo, and for a time the two men spoke in Portuguese. The discussion seemed to grow a little heated; it seemed to Christine that Felipe had put forward a proposition and was having difficulty in making the older man agree to it. At last Gustavo paused to think over the matter, and a slow grin overspread his face. Leaning across, he gave Felipe a thump on the back that nearly knocked him out of his chair; then he threw himself back and laughed long and heartily.

'Please to tell the Senhor your father,' Felipe said, turning to Christine, 'that it will be good if he wait until tomorrow.'

'If—?'

'It will be good if for one more night you stay there. For one more night, not pay; for one more night, wait.'

'We wanted to leave today,' Christine said.

Felipe relayed this statement to Gustavo, who leaned forward and joined his hands together beseechingly and seemed to second Felipe's proposal that nothing should be done until next day.

'Why not?' Christine asked. 'What's to be gained by waiting a day or a night?'

Felipe raised his shoulders as high as his ears, spread his hands wide and looked the picture of man who didn't know.

'But there must be a reason for waiting,' Christine persisted.

'Perhaps yes, perhaps no,' said Felipe. 'I

think of something, but perhaps no good. If no good, tomorrow you pay, tomorrow you come here.'

No more could be got out of him or out of Gustavo. The meeting broke up, and Josefina came out and begged Christine to step upstairs and assure herself that the rooms were ready for their return. When at last she left the Pensão, Maria de Fatima was detailed to escort her to the end of the lane, but Felipe was not permitted to escort Maria de Fatima.

On reaching the café, Christine found her parents waiting for her with the Colonel and with Charles, the latter having left his aunt at home and come back to more congenial company.

'Bad business, you all getting caught like that,' the Colonel told Christine when they had exchanged greetings. 'Been saying to your parents that if only I'd thought of putting in a word of warning, you might have been on your guard. Too late now, unfortunately.'

'Did you get the rooms?' Mr. Channing asked.

'From tomorrow,' Christine said.

'That only leaves you one more day to put in with the Baronesa,' the Colonel pointed out. 'Tell you what—why don't you all come and dine with us? Wish I'd thought of it before. Too late to fix up lunch, but come and dine; that'll get you out of the house. Yes, come along about eight. Nothing elaborate, you know; just pot luck.'

Mrs. Channing thanked him and accepted, but Mr. Channing was looking thoughtful.

'There must be some people,' he said to the Colonel, 'who've decided to stick it out at the Baronesa's. If I pay that bill, I'm entitled to a month's board and lodging for myself and my family. If we stayed, and made a point of being in for every meal—'

'—you'd have a stiff account for extras at the end of your stay,' said the Colonel. 'She'd give you out-of-season delicacies and explain—later—that of course they weren't included in your bill. She'd have a fire lit in the public rooms and charge you a sum that would be enough to heat that Palace over there. It's been tried before. Everything's been tried. There's only one thing that can put her out of business, and that's if her reputation travels far enough to keep people out of her house. But I'll take a bet with you that if you leave, within a week or less there'll be another set of victims roped in to take your place. If you intended to stay on there, why did you make enquiries about your rooms at the Pombal?'

'Because my first instinct was to get out at once. Since then, I've been thinking it over and—'

'No, you haven't,' said the Colonel. 'You've simply come out of shock and you're trying to stand up and hit back. Better men than you have had a go. You don't suppose, do you, that

135

a woman can carry on a business on these lines and not be able to deal with every kind of comeback? She hurts people in their softest part—their pockets; naturally they react in a variety of ways, all of which she's learned to cope with. If you tried to stick it out for a month, it'd get on your nerves to such an extent that it'd make a wreck of you. Pay up and clear out, that's my advice.'

'I dare say you're right,' acknowledged Mr. Channing unwillingly.

'Of course I am. Go back and start packing, and I'll expect you to dinner.' He turned to Charles. 'You too,' he said.

'Me?' Charles sounded gratified. 'Well, thanks very much. I—'

'To make the numbers even,' said the Colonel.

Raising his hat, he turned and left them. Charles went reluctantly to lunch with his aunt, and the Channings walked back to the Quinta de Narvão.

'I don't suppose,' Mr. Channing said as they neared the gate, 'that she'll show herself for lunch. She'll keep out of our way.'

But when they were walking through the house, a loud and cheerful voice hailed them from the terrace. The Baronesa, lying at ease on a long chair, waved one of the newspapers she was reading, and held up some new magazines to Mrs. Channing.

'Hello, hello, so you come back from your

walk,' she said gaily. 'Come, sit down; you must be tired. Sit down and I shall order some drinks before lunch.'

'No. Oh no, thank you,' Mr. Channing said hastily, his mind on the column marked Extras. 'Just had drinks, thank you.'

'I myself had to go out this morning to see some friends,' said the Baronesa. 'It was only just now that I came back. Did you meet the Colonel, this friend of yours?'

'Yes. As a matter of fact,' Mrs. Channing said, 'we've promised to go and dine there tonight. I hope—'

'Tonight? Ah, this is very fortunate!' the Baronesa exclaimed. 'Just now I was worrying because I myself have promised to dine with friends in Lisbon, and I did not wish to leave you all alone. But now this is good: you too will be out.'

Mr. Channing, feeling himself unable to adopt the Baronesa's bland forgetfulness of the morning's interview in the study, went up to his room to await the summons to lunch. Christine followed him, but Mrs. Channing seated herself near the Baronesa and took up one of the magazines.

'He is upset, your husband,' she heard the Baronesa say. 'This morning, I gave him a shock, yes?'

'Yes. I've always found,' Mrs. Channing said quietly, 'that purse-holders like a little preparation before being presented with large bills. It would have been better, before giving my husband his account, to have said a word or two to me.'

She was surprised and pleased to note that her words left the Baronesa, for a few moments, without anything to say. Then she rallied.

'Preparation? He said to me—did he tell you this?—that he thought that in inviting you, I had thought only of friendship.'

'Isn't that what you wanted him to think?' enquired Mrs. Channing.

There was no hostility in her tone. Disarmed, the Baronesa stared at her for a moment or two and then answered frankly.

'I shall tell you something,' she said. 'Whenever I ask people to come, I say to myself that surely, one day, somebody will say to me, when they enter my house and see for themselves what I give them: "But all this luxury for strangers, people whom you do not know?" Nobody, I assure you, nobody has ever said this. If they did, I would admit that yes, I make a little charge. It is a matter of astonishment to me how much people can take when they imagine that it is free. Then you ask them to pay, and immediately they have business which calls them away. You and your husband, too, are going to leave; this I can see quite plainly.'

'I suppose that's how most people react,' Mrs. Channing said.

138

'React? When one has a bill to pay,' the Baronesa said, 'there is no reaction except to sit down and write a cheque, isn't it?'

'Don't you ever make any concession?'

'Concession?' repeated the Baronesa in a loud, angry voice. 'Do I—'

'No, I thought not.'

'Are you going to say to me that I have not given you everything without stint?'

'At a price,' said Mrs. Channing. 'Why do they keep on saying that the best things in life are free?'

'You may indeed ask this,' said the Baronesa grimly. 'I myself can answer by saying another question: Shall this house, this way of living, this food, this service, this garden with its flowers and its fruit and its beauty—shall all this be free? Are those beds in your rooms, with their silk canopies, are these servants, are these free? Are the sofas, the chairs, the tapestries, the silver, the crystal, the pictures, the beautiful ornaments, are these free? The carpets, the curtains, all so beautiful; the cushions that you lean against, these terrace appointments, the dinner and the breakfast and the tea services of china, so exquisite—are these free? No! See if you will,' proceeded the Baronesa passionately, 'examine if you wish, my bills. See, if you will, my details of expenditure, my accounts daily for food and wine, my accounts monthly for servants, for petrol, for car, for heating, for lighting. Free? I can tell you,

Madame, that I feel sometimes that I have a hundred hands, each one of them handing money, money, money—to this one, to the other. Pay, pay, pay. If I pay out, shall not others pay in? This is what people do not understand. Even your husband. I say nothing to hurt your feelings, but is he not an example of those others who expect that I shall pay all this for their pleasure? Is this reasonable? Is this just? If I offer a perfection of living—and who shall challenge this?—am I to do it without recompense? I, who since my husband died have nothing but what I earned for myself? for yes! it is earning! Do I not work for this? You, a housewife, must see the truth. Does this beauty, this cleanliness, this matchless service, does it come of itself? You know that it does not. You know that it means ceaseless vigilance, ceaseless attention to all the details of it, eyes here, eyes there to notice, to correct, to punish. My servants—did they come to me in this way, perfect? You know better. You, Madame, are something one does not often meet with—you are a person who sees what is behind. And you see that what is behind this perfection is myself, with my work and my energy. If life has good things which are free, then go, I say, and enjoy them. For myself, nothing that I love is free—but this is my life, and I cannot, I will not live in any other way. I must have, I will have all this that you see around you. No, Madame! For me, the best

140

things in life are far from free! They are costly; my God! how costly!'

She stopped, her bosom heaving with passion. She turned from Mrs. Channing and stared over the low stone balustrade, her expression one of brooding. Mrs. Channing, watching her, said nothing for a time. Then she put another question.

'Is it really worth it?' she asked.

The Baronesa turned slowly to face her.

'Worth it? You mean is it too much work, too much planning, too much—'

'What I meant was, wouldn't you be as happy if it were all on a rather smaller scale?'

'How can I have this smaller scale? This is my house. I cannot make it smaller; I cannot take away rooms. And if I could, I would not. If there is perfection in this world, it is here in this house, in this garden. To have it, to keep it, I do not mind working, I do not mind anything. It is not easy to find people to come, month after month and year after year—but I find them. It is a challenge. Can you say that I deceive my guests? Did I once say to you All this is free? No. You did not ask, because you, like all the others, took it for granted. If you had asked, I would have told you the truth: you must pay. For if you do not pay, I cannot live.'

A gong sounded, but for some moments the Baronesa did not move. Then she rose and stood looking down at Mrs. Channing.

'You are an unusual guest, Madame,' she

141

told her. 'Almost, I could say, unique. You are the first who has ever seen my problems.'

'My trouble has always been,' Mrs. Channing said, 'that I can see both sides of every question.'

'Trouble? That is a gift, Madame; a very unusual gift.'

Mrs. Channing rose and prepared to follow her into lunch.

'I don't think it's a gift,' she said. 'If it is, it came from a very wicked fairy.'

CHAPTER SIX

The Baronesa drove away at about six o'clock; two hours later, the Channings summoned a taxi and went to dine at the Bell-Burtons.

Mr. and Mrs. Channing had not been in the mood, on their previous visit, to take in any details, but they thought it unnecessary for the Colonel to explain, as he did on their arrival, that he had designed the house himself; it looked exactly the kind of house they would have expected him to design, being plain, compact, square and solid. It was set in a pine wood, and the neat drive was bordered by flowers that stood up like troops at attention. The Colonel clearly had none of Gustavo's grow-as-you-please attitude to Nature; his garden looked as though he marched it out every morning and left it in formation.

Mrs. Bell-Burton, standing on the steps to receive the guests, was as plain as her house. Mrs. Channing remembered her as a somewhat blowzy bride, but thirty years of life with the Colonel had tidied her up. Her lack of tact, however, was as much in evidence as ever. She offered a cheek to Mrs. Channing and told her she was looking out of sorts, shook hands with Christine and said she was almost but not quite as pretty as her sisters, raised her voice when greeting Mr. Channing, as though the intervening years had made him deaf, and then led the way indoors.

Here, the same rather bleak order prevailed. If the Colonel and his wife read books, they were hidden from sight. If Mrs. Bell-Burton sewed, or embroidered, or wrote letters or cut out dresses or subscribed to magazines, no evidence of these activities could be seen; so bare was the drawing-room of any personal touch that the visitors might have been inspecting a house that was to be let furnished. There was not even, to Mrs. Channing's surprise, any sign that there were three young children living in the house; asking whether they had left, she learned that they had not, but were kept strictly to their own rooms. Their visit, she gathered from their grandmother, was not proving a great success; they were accustomed to speaking Dutch to their parents, French to their father's French mother, and Portuguese to the servants. English, which the Colonel and his wife persisted in regarding as their mother tongue, they spoke little, and badly, so that the Colonel's attempts to drill them into English ways were proving abortive.

Charles Granger, arriving a little late, was reproved by the Colonel and then ordered to busy himself preparing drinks. He led him into the dining-room, showed him a row of bottles, told him what everybody would like, and then returned to settle down beside Mr. Channing for a chat about old days. Mrs. Bell-Burton, seated beside Mrs. Channing on the sofa, began a conversation in the brisk voice which, united with her now neat and businesslike appearance, led strangers to the erroneous conclusion that she was a woman of sense.

'It's nice to see you all again,' she said, 'though I must say I was dreading it, when I heard you were coming. After all this time, you never know what people are going to look like, do you? You're still living in the same house in England?'

'Yes.'

'You don't find it too large now that three of them are off your hands? I don't suppose you can get servants?'

'I've got dailies; I manage all right on the whole. It must be nice to have all these maids out here.'

'My dear, I could do twice the work in half

144

the time. The trouble is that I can't afford to pay high wages, so as soon as I've trained a girl, off she goes.'

She paused to take a drink from the tray Charles was holding, sipped it, shuddered and made a grimace.

'Oh *strong!*' she exclaimed. 'Goodness, I couldn't drink *that!*'

The Colonel, taking a glass and sampling the contents pronounced in an angry tone that the mixture was enough to knock any ordinary man off his feet. Charles was marched back to the dining-room and told to water down the mixture.

'What I always say,' he explained, settling down at last beside Christine with a mutinous expression, 'is that the first drink's got to be potent. You've got to get the party going, and you can't do it on wish-wash. The duller, the stronger, is my rule. If there'd been half a dozen beautiful girls present, instead of only one, the men wouldn't have known what they were drinking, but when there's just one young couple and all the rest—'

He saw the direction in which he was headed, and to Christine's disappointment, left the sentence unfinished.

The wish-wash was handed round and before there was time for a second drink, a diminutive maid with curly black hair, big black eyes and dark-brown skin appeared at the door and announced dinner.

145

The company filed into a dining-room whose chief decoration was pots of ferns set round the walls. The Colonel pulled out Mrs. Channing's chair and settled her into it.

'Haven't got a leg, have you?' he asked anxiously. 'Nice table, this, but you have to be careful where you put the chairs, or people sit down and give their knees a thundering great crack and—There! Don't say I didn't warn you, Bruce.'

Mr. Channing, doing his best to make light of his agony, reflected morosely that liar and cheat as the Baronesa undoubtedly was, she didn't put booby traps under her dining-table, didn't offer guests stale cigarettes and didn't whisk a drink away to bring it back swamped. Like Mrs. Channing, he was recalling facts about the Colonel and his wife that he had forgotten, the chief being that their parties had been, in the past, affairs at all costs to be avoided.

Time, he had once read somewhere, could do great disservice. It had certainly done great disservice to the Colonel's conversation. Either he himself had grown intolerant or the Colonel had become a prosy old bore.

He put uncharitable thoughts out of his head and tried to remember only the Colonel's kindness, but the dinner did nothing to help him. The soup was oily, the meat tough and the vegetables cold. Between courses, the Colonel and his wife kept up an unceasing flow of reminiscences. They recalled incidents long forgotten, of no great interest to Mr. and Mrs. Channing and of no interest whatsoever to Christine and Charles. They began an account, stopped to argue about its exact date, asked for news of people Mr. Channing had not set eyes on for twenty years, recalled with relish the foibles and idiosyncrasies of old acquaintances and forgot their guests in recreating a past which had obviously been more active, more colourful, more varied than their present uneventful existence.

The meat plates were cleared away; a glass dish containing a white mess was placed in front of Mrs. Bell-Burton.

'I like to serve the pudding myself,' she explained. 'I always make it; I can't get Portuguese servants to understand English puddings. This is tipsy: my husband's favourite.'

The guests were handed plates on which a milky stream oozed from soggy sponge cakes. They stirred it, said it was delicious, hid as much as possible under their spoons and filed back to the drawing-room for coffee. Mr. Channing, bracing himself to endure another hour of the Colonel's company, recalled firmly his good nature, marshalled every past instance of his kindness, pitied him for being condemned to live with Mrs. Bell-Burton and reminded himself that it was the Colonel who had placed them at the Pensão Pombal—but it

147

was no easier, at the end of this summary of good points, to endure more of the reminiscences or to simulate interest in old photograph albums containing snapshots of himself which, for fear of his children's ridicule, he had been careful to suppress. The photographs, had, however, the effect of enlivening the evening for Christine.

The albums having been looked through, Mrs. Bell-Burton told fortunes and the Colonel did card tricks. Then he opened an ancient cottage piano and asked Christine to play.

'I gave it up when I was eleven,' she told him.

'Your parents shouldn't have allowed you to,' the Colonel said. 'Do you know that before I was eight, I was locked into the schoolroom for an hour every day, to practise the piano?'

'Then *you* must play to *us*,' said Christine.

'Well ... If you insist ...'

The Colonel sat down and played, and the visitors gave every appearance of listening with absorbed interest. Mrs. Channing wished he had thought of it before; it was a rest from reminiscences. Mr. Channing thought that even giving the Baronesa a cheque could be hardly more painful than this. Charles fell asleep; Christine thought of Gustavo and Felipe and wondered what difference the proposed delay in paying the Baronesa could make in the situation. She had thought of recounting the details of the verandah meeting

148

to her mother, and had decided against it; she knew as yet little about the Portuguese character, but she had heard that one of its aspects was the habit of cheering the dejected by making rosy promises that could not possibly be fulfilled.

They rose at last to take their leave of the Colonel and his wife.

'Nice to have had you,' the Colonel said, when the taxi had been telephoned for and had arrived. 'It's a great pity your introduction to Portugal has been so unfortunate. I was going to persuade you to come out permanently. You'd be very happy here, once you settled down. Climate's damp from October to May, of course, and that strong breeze we get all summer gives some people headaches, and I dare say a lot of people will tell you that Sintra sits under a perpetual cloud, but that only makes it cool. You ought to think about it.'

Promising to think about it, the Channings, with Charles, drove away.

'I don't know about you, but I'm hellishly hungry,' Charles said as soon as they had rounded the curve of the road. 'Jolly kind to have us and all that, but all I've got inside me is some soup and a bit of hard potato. I would have had a bash at the meat, but I've got the sort of teeth that keep chipping off if I'm not careful. Don't want to seem ungrateful, or to abuse hospitality or anything of that sort, but I'm going to shake up my aunt's maids and tell 'em to feed me. I suppose you wouldn't care to join me?'

They said that it would be better if they didn't disturb his aunt's maids. They dropped him at a low, long, pink-and-white house on whose walls hung lanterns still hospitably alight and then they drove on to the Baronesa's house, to find a maid and a man waiting for them, their beds invitingly prepared, and on small wagons in each room, hot and cold drinks and a variety of small, savoury sandwiches. Mr. Channing, eating his fill, poured himself out a whisky and drank it recklessly; she'd slap on another staggering bill for extras, of course, but at this moment he could almost ... almost ... feel that he was getting value for money.

Mrs. Channing went in to say good night to Christine, and found her lying in bed looking pensive.

'Tired?' she asked.

'No. I was just wishing I'd studied languages.'

Her mother sat on the end of the bed.

'I wish you'd studied anything,' she said. 'I don't think any girls as intelligent as you and your sisters ever went through school and came out knowing less.'

'Neville was the bright one.'

'He wasn't. He was just the only one who understood that school was a place where you could learn—if you wanted to. If ever money

150

was wasted, it was on your education, and on your sisters'.'

'Well, now I'm sorry,' Christine said. 'If I'd paid attention, I might have picked up a word or two of Portuguese and been able to understand what people were talking about.'

'Do you want to stay out here, or go home?'

Christine yawned and slipped down between the sheets.

'Stay, on the whole,' she said. 'Out here, I think about James—underneath—most of the time, but at home I'd think about him all the time. Seems funny to think you might have felt like this once about Father. Don't tell me he was a passionate lover.'

'He was a faithful husband; let's hope you can say the same about James after as many years. Good night, darling.'

'Don't go for a minute. I've got some news.'

'Good news?'

'Wonderful news. Katherine Staples is out here.'

Mrs. Channing gazed at her in astonishment.

'James's cousin ... here in Portugal?'

Christine made a contented sound of assent.

'Staying in a Quinta near Sintra. Charles told me. I didn't know how much I'd been worrying about her until I heard she was out of the reach of James's grandfather.'

'How long—'

'Three weeks, Charles said. Her mother

151

breeds dogs.'

'No connection with Great Danes—'

'—the Baronesa brought out? The long arm can't be as long as that.'

'I suppose not.'

Mrs. Channing went back to her room, but as her husband was asleep, she was unable to give him Christine's news.

There was no sign of the Baronesa the next morning. The Channings ate their breakfast under a blue-and-white-striped canopy on the terrace, the food kept hot in a large, portable electric oven plugged into the wall. There was porridge, a variety of other cereals, bacon and eggs, kidneys, scrambled eggs with or without tomato, omelettes plain and omelettes filled with mushrooms. There were hot rolls, toast timed to a nicety by a little uniformed boy at a side table, marmalade and honey and yoghurt and coffee and cream and pitchers of hot milk and little golden hot scones and an array of tiny tumblers filled with orange and lemon and grapefruit and pineapple and tomato juice. It was impossible not to acknowledge that though the Baronesa asked much, she gave much. But not, Mr. Channing felt, the bill burning a hole in his pocket, not enough. When the Baronesa came downstairs, he would accompany her to her study, count out the cash the Colonel had kindly let him have, ask for the passports, and go upstairs and pack. Then they would order a taxi and drive to the Pensão Pombal, which they should never have left.

Christine put aside her napkin at last, and gave a sigh of repletion.

'If I said I wasn't sorry to be leaving this food,' she said, 'it wouldn't be true.' She got up and, walking round the table, ruffled her father's hair. 'All the same, I'm sorry we've been had for mugs.'

Mr. Channing said nothing. He was resolving that when they went home, he would suggest to Madeleine that perhaps breakfast could be stretched a little—kidney, for example, as well as eggs and bacon, and perhaps a bit of fish to follow. The Baronesa had cheated him, humiliated him, insulted him, robbed him—but she had given him one or two ideas about food that he hoped to incorporate into the menus at home.

When she appeared at last, it was not from her bedroom but in the car, returning from an early errand. They saw her get out, and Mrs. Channing and Christine took in the details of her beautiful, black-and-white suit, fresh, uncrushable, impeccably cut. Her manner, when she looked up and waved to them, when she joined them on the terrace and ordered fresh coffee and distributed an armful of papers and magazines, was as cheerful, her voice as loud and confident as ever. 'You have finished already,' she said. 'I meant to be back in time to join you at breakfast. But I had to go

153

out early—very early—and I did not even stop to leave my apologies with you. You enjoyed your visit to your friends?'

They had, lied Mrs. Channing, enjoyed it very much.

'While you were there,' the Baronesa said, seating herself in a long chair and leaning back, 'I thought very much about you all. What a pity, I said to myself, that when people are charming like you, so good, so delightful, we should have ... should we say a little misunderstanding between us? I said to myself that after all, perhaps I was to blame for not at once saying to you: Here you see me outwardly gay, outwardly of elegant appearance, but inside I am unhappy for money, inside I am always uneasy. This I tried to explain yesterday to you, isn't it?' She turned to ask Mrs. Channing. 'I tried to tell you that here— alas!—is beauty that must be paid for. But when I asked your husband to pay he was surprised, shocked, upset. So in the night I said to myself that today I would come to you at breakfast and I would make for you a proposition.'

She paused, looking round at her listeners. There was nothing to be seen in their expressions, however, but varying degrees of suspicion.

'I think I ought to tell you,' Mr. Channing said, 'that we are leaving...'

'Oh, this I have guessed, but I beg you to

listen to what I have to say!' The Baronesa paused once more, this time to pour out her coffee. 'What I am going to say to you, this proposition, it is this: I am going to say to you to pay for these days that you have spent with me, but if you wish to leave, then you shall not pay for this month that you booked. Perhaps you did not realize all that my house would offer, and for this reason you were not prepared to pay what I charged you. Very well. Now I say that you shall pay only for your days here. This morning, I went out early into Lisbon to see a friend of mine and I begged her to take you in her house, which is not, of course, like mine, but which is less cost. She said it was difficult, but for me, she will do it. From today, you may go there. All is arranged, all is now friendly, all will end in a happy way. All it is now, is to pay me the money for these days.'

There was a long silence. Mr. Channing needed time to take in all that had been said; his wife and Christine waited for his reactions. The Baronesa sipped her coffee.

'As a matter of fact,' Mr. Channing began at last, 'I was about—'

'Ah, but shall we not now stop saying I-did, you-did, he-did?' enquired the Baronesa in brisk protest. 'Shall we not say only that when I have had my coffee, we shall go together to my study and you shall write your cheque for me and then we shall part with on both sides friendliness? There will—this I must say at once, because I do not wish you again to accuse me of misleading—there are certain little things extra; for these it is only right that I should ask you to pay, isn't it? But from today, from this breakfast which I hope you have enjoyed ... nothing!' She finished her coffee and looked at them all with an expectant smile. 'This is the happy ending, no?'

'I must say,' Mr. Channing said, 'that—'

'Yes,' said Mrs. Channing.

The Baronesa turned to her, beaming.

'Ah, so! Yesterday I said to you how rare you are! You are one who understands. That is what I said to my friend Lydia when I saw her this morning: Madame, I told her, is charming. She is looking forward to meeting you. Lydia, like myself, has the misfortune to have to share her house with strangers—but her house is smaller, her servants fewer, her food not as exquisite as I hope I may say mine is always. I have arranged everything with her for you. She—'

'I'm afraid,' Mr. Channing broke in, 'you put yourself to trouble for nothing. I would like to settle with you, and then we should like to—'

A frown had appeared on the Baronesa's brow.

'This is not a polite way to meet kindness, I would say,' she said in an annoyed tone. 'I say to you first: I will cancel for you the days that you do not stay here. Next I say I have arranged for you—'

'We are going back,' Mr. Channing said, 'to the Pensão Pombal.'

'But they will not have your rooms any more! You gave them up and came to me to—'

'We saw them and asked if they would have us back. They said they could.'

The Baronesa sat for some moments deep in thought.

'You intend to stay on here—here in Sintra?' she enquired at last. 'For how long?'

'We shall stay at the Pensão Pombal,' Mr. Channing told her, 'until I've managed to fix up our homeward passages.'

'But why do you stay in discomfort? Why do you not go to my friend in Lisbon? You have seen enough in Sintra, isn't it? In Lisbon, you would have a change and—'

'We have made definite arrangements at the Pensão,' said Mr. Channing.

The Baronesa appeared to make some further calculations, and then shrugged.

'Very well. It will make it awkward for me to tell my friend that you have changed your minds and will not stay with her after all. I do not think she will be pleased, since at this moment she is going to trouble to prepare rooms for you.' She rose and waved Mr. Channing indoors. 'You and I will come to my study,' she said. 'You have my little account?'

Mr. Channing produced it from his pocket.

157

'I must change it, isn't it? There is some to add. But I am sure you are happy that I am going to mark only until today. You are going to pay me in escudos? I always—'

Her voice died away. Mrs. Channing and Christine were left alone.

'I wonder,' Christine said slowly after a time, 'whether this has anything to do with Felipe?'

She saw the lack of comprehension in her mother's eyes and gave her a brief summary of yesterday's conversation with Gustavo and Felipe on the verandah of the Pensão Pombal.

'What possible connection could there be between him and the Baronesa?' Mrs. Channing asked at the end of the recital.

'Well, it's a bit odd, isn't it? *He* says wait until tomorrow, and *she* skips up to us today knocking nine-tenths off our bill. Didn't the Colonel tell you that nobody had ever got off without paying the full amount? Why should she let us off? She knew she'd trapped us. She didn't even know we meant to pay her and clear out today.'

'She wanted us out,' Mrs. Channing said slowly. 'She was going, in effect, to turn us out.'

'Turn us over—to her friend Lydia. It's fishy, isn't it, whichever way you look at it?'

'There's something behind it, but I hardly think it's anything to do with this young man called Felipe.'

'Well, guessing won't get us anywhere. What

158

do we do now—go upstairs and pack?'

'We sit here and it all gets done for us. Enjoy it while you can; it'll never happen again.'

When they were ready to leave, their luggage was brought down, a taxi drove up, and from nowhere appeared a group of servants, to perform the last services and then to stand back, impassive but expectant.

'What I forgot to tell you,' the Baronesa said in an audible aside to Mr. Channing, 'is that on your bill I did not put for service. Usually, when it seems that people are not aware of what is right to do in this matter, I add fifteen per cent. But for you I did not.'

Mr. Channing handed his wife and daughter into the taxi, took from his pocket a note of very moderate size and stepped up to the servant first in line.

'Divide that,' he said clearly, 'between you.'

He bowed to the Baronesa, got into the taxi and gave a firm order.

'Pen-sow Pom-barl.'

Little was said on the way. Mr. Channing sat thinking matters over and came to the conclusion that the best thing they could do would be to go home as soon as possible. They had, by some extraordinary and unlooked-for turn of luck, been delivered from the Baronesa's worst demands, but the fact remained that he had got through a great deal of money in a very short time. The thing now was to get home and—as far as he was

159

concerned—stay at home. There had been a time when he had been able to hold his own in the world, but standards were not what they were. Decent people had either to give up the struggle against the sharks, or grow tough enough to fight them. Men like himself had better recognize that they were too old to learn new fighting tactics, and keep out of the ring.

Mrs. Channing followed her husband's train of thought without difficulty, and sat preparing arguments to delay their departure for at least a week. They had paid their fares, they were here, Sintra was beautiful, the weather was perfect and there was still a lot to see. The interlude at the Quinta de Narvão had shaken them all, but it was over, and running home wouldn't bring back the money they had spent. They had come in the first place for Christine's benefit, and for Christine's benefit they should stay on for a time.

Christine, knowing that her father would want to go and her mother would like to stay, decided that she would enter the contest on her mother's side. It would be silly to go home so soon; they should stay on and begin to enjoy themselves. Perhaps Charles could borrow his aunt's car for a little sight-seeing; it was too much to hope that her father could be induced to hire a car.

Their arrival at the Pombal was in the nature of a reception. The work had been done in anticipation of their arrival; everybody was on

160

the look-out for them. Gustavo hurried to open the door of the taxi, his wife and daughters carried the luggage into the house, the dogs barked, the cats peered round the bushes, Maria de Fatima carried wine out to the tables and pulled out the chairs. The taxi driver was given a drink and sent on his way. Mrs. Channing, followed by Maria-Helena, Maria-Jose and Maria-Innocencia, went upstairs to do the unpacking. She came down again to join her husband and Christine on the verandah and pour out the coffee that Gustavo's wife placed before her.

They had just finished it when into the courtyard came a very old, very noisy, very well-preserved car that might have taken its place at a Veteran Car Rally. Out of it stepped the Colonel.

'Meant to be here when you arrived,' he said, taking off his Panama hat and joining the Channings on the verandah. 'Wanted to be here to cheer you up. Well, well, best thing now is to forget all about it. Worse things could have happened. It's been a nasty knock, but it's better to take it on the pocket than on the head.'

'We only paid,' said Mr. Channing, 'for the length of our stay.'

'What I always say,' proceeded the Colonel, unheeding, 'is that a bit of philosophy ...' He paused, staring. '*What* was that you said just now?'

161

'I said we only had to pay, in the end, for the days we'd spent there.'

'Nonsense,' said the Colonel. 'There's some mistake. What I mean to say is, there's something ... No, I don't understand it. You told me, didn't you, that she'd billed you for a month?'

'Yes. But she let me off.'

'Let you off?' echoed the Colonel in a dazed voice. 'Let you *off*? You must be joking. The Baronesa never lets anybody off anything. Sure you've got it right? Bill receipted?'

'Yes. We only paid for the days we were there.'

There was a pause.

'I don't like it,' the Colonel said decisively at last. 'I don't like it at all. Did you get your passports?'

'Yes.'

'Did you get all your things? Your luggage?'

'Yes.'

'Did you see it packed yourselves?'

'No. But it's all there,' Mrs. Channing said. 'I've just unpacked it.'

'I don't understand it.' The Colonel shook his head. 'I've been here sixteen years,' he said slowly, 'and in all that time, nobody has ever got off scot-free. They—'

'Scot-free?' Mr. Channing spoke with heat. 'Do you call that bill I paid for those days we were there scot-free? For two of those days we were out for lunch and tea and dinner, and I

162

had to pay, and pay through the nose, for eating at restaurants I'd never asked to go to. Scot-free?'

'You didn't have to pay for the month she'd billed you for.'

'I had to pay an iniquitous bill for what she called extras. Extras! Why, the—'

'There are thirty days in a month. You paid, say, for five. Five into thirty goes six times,' the Colonel pointed out. 'Multiply what you paid by six, and add a tenfold bill for imaginary extras, and then you'll agree that you got off scot-free. You can take it from me that there's something behind it. I assure you that the Baronesa doesn't act from philanthropic motives. If she hasn't kept a nasty surprise up her sleeve, I'll eat this hat of mine. Sure you've got your return tickets?'

'I've got them,' Mrs. Channing said.

The Colonel rose.

'Well, it's a mystery,' he said. 'I'm glad if it's true, of course, but I've got a strong feeling there's a bit missing.'

'She tried to book rooms for us with a friend of hers,' Mrs. Channing said.

'Ah! Now we're getting somewhere!' said the Colonel. 'She wanted you out. That means that she'd found somebody she wanted to rope in. Somebody she *had* roped in, in fact; she wouldn't have let you off unless she'd been quite sure. She tried to push you off to Lisbon, you say?'

163

'Yes.'

'Then she's got somebody else and wanted you right out of the way. Now *that* makes more sense. I'll go and walk round the square and see if I can't pick up anything on the bush telegraph. If I do, I'll come back and tell you. But mark my words, that's the explanation: she's netted some other fish.'

Mr. Channing accompanied him to his car, and Christine looked at her mother.

'See what I mean?' she asked. 'There *is* something.'

'But not necessarily anything to do with Gustavo and—what was his name?'

'Felipe. If only I could talk this language, I'd ask Gustavo a few questions. I've got a feeling there's some connection somewhere.'

Mrs. Channing said nothing. She was not greatly interested in the means whereby they had escaped; it was enough that they were free of the Baronesa. They were back here, transplanted in rougher soil, back in this homely setting. Here, there was none of the well-organized peace that had characterized the Quinta de Narvão; there was noise, and bustle, but anybody with a gift for sitting and looking could find interest enough. Mrs. Channing, aware that life had lately offered her little opportunity for the exercise of the gift, leaned back in her chair and gave herself up to enjoyment. She listened to Maria de Fatima singing, in a loud, sad, strident voice, a haunting *fado*. She watched the pigeons as they rose in a sudden flutter, swooped across the courtyard and settled on the roof of the stable. A donkey cart clattered into the courtyard, discharging its cargo of charcoal and clattered out. A small boy rode in on a bicycle on either side of which were large panniers filled with bread; Gustavo's wife came out, chose several loaves of varied shapes, pushed them into snow-white cotton bags and carried them into the house. Gustavo chopped wood, the girls washed the clothes and hung them up to dry, the children played. From the kitchen came delicious smells, and the splutter and hiss of frying. A little girl came on to the verandah carrying a dish of black olives.

'Happy?' Christine asked, after a time.

Mrs. Channing nodded, her eyes on her husband, who was standing near a small clay grill on which one of the little girls was grilling fresh, whole sardines; he was watching the operation with great interest, and accepted one of the crisp, blackened fish to sample. Something about him made her realize that he, like herself, was beginning to feel at home in this simple, carefree atmosphere. Perhaps he would not, after all, be anxious to hurry away.

Gustavo's wife came out to tell them that when they were ready, the food was also ready. They turned toward the dining-room and saw their table covered in a fresh white cloth on which were thick plates and a bread-filled basket.

'Never tasted anything like those sardines,' Mr. Channing told them, taking his place and drawing up his chair expectantly. 'Did you see how they were doing them, Madeleine?'

'Yes.'

'They don't even clean them; straight out of the sea and grilled just as they come. I dare say we'll be having some now.'

But first there was thick vegetable soup. After that came a flat dish piled high with the grilled sardines. They began by counting how many they ate; later, they thought it best to eat without counting. They tried, without success, to do justice to the fried veal that followed, and to the cheese, and to the cherries and oranges and figs.

It seemed a long walk back to the verandah. Sitting in a shady corner, they drank strong coffee, and Mr. Channing came out of a long reverie to make an observation.

'Extraordinary,' he said. 'Can't think how they do it.'

'Do what?' Christine enquired.

'Do it for the price. Of course it's simple and it's shabby; no money spent on appearances— but that was a splendid meal. Pity one can't get fresh sardines at home. We could have bought one of those little grills and taken it back, perhaps. Best to grill out of doors, I understood them to say.'

They tried to imagine Mr. Channing out in

the garden, grilling fresh sardines, and Mrs. Channing marvelled at a man who, professing to detest garlic, had since his arrival in the country been eating it without protest—without, she thought, knowing that it was present in the food. At the Quinta de Narvão, it had been used with discretion, so that perhaps it was not to be wondered at that he had failed to detect its presence; here, however, the veal had had small incisions into which tiny pieces of garlic had been thrust; he had eaten a salad from which waves of garlic had risen and filled the air. He was sitting now breathing out strong fumes—but it would not do to tell him so.

They fought off the inertia that threatened to overpower them. Mr. Channing longed to go up and stretch himself on the vast bed. Mrs. Channing would have liked to put a chair out in the courtyard and doze. Instead, they decided to go for a walk. Having drunk some more strong coffee, they wandered through the pine woods and climbed up a steep track and along a ridge that gave a beautiful view of the surrounding countryside.

They walked back to the Pensão and sat on the verandah; Gustavo's wife brought them strong, well-made tea. They had just finished it when the Colonel's car drove into the courtyard and stopped with a cough and a shudder. They walked down to meet him, but he did not get out of the car. Leaning out, he spoke to them.

'Can't stop,' he said. 'Just came along to tell you I was right.'

'What about?' Christine asked.

'Why, about that old shark of a Baronesa. I knew there was something behind it. Didn't I tell you she wouldn't have let you off like that unless she was on to somebody else? Well, she was. The reason you got out was simply that she wanted somebody else in. You can thank your lucky stars she did. She's a wonder, say what you like. A shark, of course; but clever, damned clever.'

'You mean she's arranging for somebody to take our places?' Mrs. Channing asked.

'Arranging? Arranged! She's got 'em. They're in. You're out of the net because she found bigger fish to fry. When you drove out, she drove into Lisbon to fetch them. She brought them back with her and installed them; brought them back, bag and baggage, in time for lunch. I knew I'd find something behind that let-off you had.'

'It's a pity,' Mr. Channing said, 'that somebody couldn't have warned them.'

The Colonel started the engine and shouted over the noise.

'Don't worry too much about them,' he yelled. 'They sound as if they can afford it. English. Landed gentry Castle up in Northumberland and what-all. Sorry I can't stop; just wanted you to know. Knew you'd be

168

interested. 'Bye. I'll bring Thelma along soon.
'Bye.'

Mrs. Channing stepped forward and
shouted a question.

'What are their names?'

'Not at all; pleasure,' yelled the Colonel.

Christine put a hand on the side of the car in
an attempt to hold it back.

'What-are-their-names?' she shouted.

'Eh? Names? Whose names?'

'Those people at the Quinta,' screamed
Christine.

'Earl and his son. No, grandson. Well, so
long.'

The car turned a wide circle. Its nose was
pointed towards the road; the Colonel was
changing gear. Christine dashed forward and
stood directly in its path and the Colonel came
to a grinding stop.

'Hey,' he shouted. 'Don't do that again.
Damned dangerous. These brakes aren't all
that good, y'know.'

'What ... are ... their ... names?' shouted
Christine.

'Whose names?'

'Those people at the Quinta.'

'Eh?'

'Those ... people ... at ...'

'Oh. I just told you.'

'You didn't. What are they *called*?'

'Called?' The Colonel took a moment to
recollect. 'Earl of Saxonford,' he shouted.

'Didn't catch the grandson's name. Out of the way, like a good girl.'

Christine stepped aside. The noise of the car rose to a deafening roar and then died away down the lane. A swirl of dust rose and slowly settled.

Christine walked across the courtyard and joined her parents. Nobody could think of anything to say. In silence, they walked together into the house.

CHAPTER SEVEN

The shock of discovering that the new guests at the Quinta de Narvão were James and his grandfather reacted on the Channings in widely different ways—but even before the first comments on the situation had been exchanged, they had all decided on the same course of action: to return at once to England.

Mr. Channing had been the first to make up his mind. As a general rule slow in taking in a situation, he had leapt now to the horrifying realization that the earl was soon to learn that the girl who had agreed to part for three months from his grandson was here in Portugal, here in Sintra, less than a mile from the Quinta de Narvão. The first conclusion that would be drawn would be that the girl's parents had deliberately thrown their daughter

170

in his grandson's way. Suspicions of that kind could later be dispelled, but nothing, in Mr. Channing's view, could ever satisfactorily efface such an impression. The humiliation he had endured at the Quinta de Narvão would be nothing, he knew, to that of being suspected by the earl of a desire to entrap James. The sooner he could remove his wife and daughter, the better.

Christine was not in a state to reason calmly; she wanted only to go to the Quinta de Narvão and confront James. It was one thing to spend the three months in England, humouring his grandfather, going about his business, submitting to some pressure to meet his cousin Katherine, to entertain her, perhaps to escort her here and there. It was quite another thing to agree to follow her all the way to Portugal in order to spend long, uninterrupted, sunny days in her society. There had been nothing in the agreement that had limited either James or herself, during the three months of separation, to any specific course of conduct or action, but ethics, she told herself bitterly, were ethics. There was, after all, a code. Anybody who couldn't see the difference between seeing his cousin at home in England, and hanging round her day after day in Sintra, was crazy. If that was what he wanted to do, let him by all means do it; she herself would go back to England and take up life where he had interrupted it.

Mrs. Channing, much more reluctantly,

reached the same conclusion as her husband and her daughter: they must leave Portugal. She did not feel that the earl's reactions were of much importance; she did not share her husband's horror of being suspected of connivance. She did not even feel certain, as Christine did, that James had come out to Portugal in order to devote himself to his cousin; all she was certain of was her inability to persuade her husband and her daughter to remain when both had such urgent reasons for leaving. It was a pity; she liked the Pensão Pombal very much indeed and would have liked to have spent some time there, but if Bruce was going to feel humiliated and if Christine was going to torment herself with mind-pictures of James in Katherine Staples's pocket, they may as well go home.

Thus she had nothing to offer in the way of opposition when Mr. Channing and Christine stated their intention of leaving.

'I'll go into Lisbon tomorrow morning and book air fares,' Mr. Channing said at the conclusion of the brief discussion. 'If there's a plane the day after tomorrow, we'll try to get on it. I'll change the sea tickets for air passages; it might mean paying a bit more, but there's no question of hanging round hoping for berths. I'll fix up places on the first plane I can.'

They had dinner in silence; Gustavo and his wife, sensing trouble, watched them anxiously. They sat for a time on the verandah and then

172

decided to go to bed.

But not, they discovered, to sleep.

They had learned something of the daily life of the Pensão Pombal; they now learned that it also had a night life. By day, there was work to be done, but once the evening meal was over, work could cease and play could begin. The Pensão, as its name proved, was not only a home but an inn; anybody was free to wander up the lane, sit on the verandah and order a glass of wine. Gustavo's three eldest daughters, though married and with homes of their own, liked to spend the evenings with their parents, bringing their children with them. The unmarried daughters, though they could not be called pretty, were clearly popular; young men liked to call on them and wander about the dark courtyard talking, or singing *fados*. Gustavo, seated with his wife on the verandah, would now and then get up and lean over the railing and count heads; if any were missing, he would storm down the steps, peer into the pine woods and roar for the wanderers. By the washing tank, Felipe and Maria de Fatima could be dimly discerned; sometimes Felipe's guitar could be heard, or Gustavo's accordion. There was talk and laughter, none of it rowdy, but all of it carrying clearly to the bedrooms above, where the English visitors were pictured lying at peace, lulled by the soft singing.

At midnight, the guests departed, Gustavo and his family went to bed and silence fell on

173

the house—and then the animals had their turn. Anybody, Mr. Channing moaned, tossing miserably on his straw mattress, anybody who thought that cocks crowed only at dawn, ought to come and spend a night at the Pensão Pombal, where the cocks began at one-fifteen and went on at three-minute intervals until daybreak. When the cocks were not crowing, the dogs were barking. They barked at themselves, they barked at their neighbours and then they joined their neighbours and barked at dogs that were barking in the distance. The female cats howled and the tomcats fought. At times, the donkey brayed—a sudden terrifying snort followed by an inhuman scream followed by a long succession of sobs.

At dawn, in a temporary lull, Mrs. Channing got up and opened the window wide and leaned out to sniff the sharp, sweet air. Behind her, her husband snored, sleeping the sleep of the exhausted. Outside the window, the pine trees looked fresh and graceful in the pale light. Soon the family of Gustavo would stir, rise, go about the day's business. The girls would begin to wash, Josefina would begin to cook. It would have been interesting to stay on for a while and learn something more of the ways in which she cooked; to watch her preparing fish and meat and the thick, delicious vegetable soups. The kitchen was not at all like the cool, green-and-white one at home in Hampshire; it

174

was hot and cluttered and hung about with ornamental wooden spoons and bunches of peppers and chilis, and smelt of a mixture of herbs, sausage and garlic. It was a pity to go away so soon, a pity to leave this friendly, smiling Portuguese atmosphere. But go they must.

Mr. Channing woke late, and unrefreshed, and over a cup of tea asked his wife to tell him what he had done to deserve these misfortunes. He had come to this country reluctantly and against his better judgment. He had been forced, almost dragged—to what? He would tell her to what. First, to be cheated. Next, to be made to appear a vulgar, cadging snob eager to catch any crumb of favour thrown by a titled stranger. Finally, to this appalling situation, which got worse whichever way you looked at it. If they walked into the Square and ran into James and his grandfather, what was the first, the only, the shocking interpretation that madman would place on their presence here? Simply that they had brought their daughter out to throw her in James's way. Oh yes, one could eventually clear the matter up; one could eventually—perhaps—convince a hot-tempered earl that they weren't after his grandson—but after that? Were they to look blank when the subject of the Baronesa came up? Wasn't it ten to one that what the Colonel called the bush telegraph would inform the earl, sooner or later, that the Channings had got out in order to let him in? Wouldn't he then see the whole thing as a plot? It was a bad dream; a nightmare. It was a pity they had ever left Hampshire.

He had intended to go into Lisbon during the morning, but his almost sleepless night, his late awakening made him decide to wait until the afternoon. After eating a lunch that his wife thought remarkably hearty for so stricken a man, he set out in a taxi to the station, there to board one of the little silvery trains that ran between Sintra and Lisbon. Mrs. Channing was left with her daughter. Warned by her husband just before his departure that he might be able to get seats on the night flight, she went upstairs, followed by Maria-Jose, Maria-Helena and Maria-Innocencia, to do the packing. Gustavo and his wife, led to believe that there had been bad news from home necessitating their speedy departure, hung about looking bereaved. The heavier suitcases were carried down and lined up in the hall, and Mrs. Channing, staring at them bleakly, found her spirits sinking to a level they seldom reached. She had, she reminded herself, persuaded her husband to come. She had been, in a sense, responsible for this disastrous holiday. She had brought him out here to expense and humiliation. But in spite of all that had happened, she did not want to go home.

It was not a cheerful afternoon. Mrs. Channing and Christine sat on the verandah

176

and Gustavo himself carried out their tea. They drank it in silence, looking out at the sun-drenched courtyard, at the scrawny hens pecking in the dust, at the girls washing and the children playing near the tank. Mrs. Channing thought of her husband, alone in a strange city, lost among strange tongues. Christine thought of James, now no doubt seated on the terrace of the Quinta de Narvão with Katherine Staples beside him and the earl rubbing his hands in the background. Even the thought of the bill that the Baronesa would shortly present brought no consolation; perhaps earls were not charged anything at all but remained honoured guests to the end of their stay. Perhaps it was only small fry like the Channings who had to pay.

'Would you,' her mother asked, 'like a walk? We could go to the station and wait for your father.'

Christine shook her head. Round any corner, she seemed to infer, there might lurk the two faces of James.

So it was that Mr. Channing, coming out of Sintra station into the late afternoon sunshine, found nobody waiting for him. But there was pleasure in the cool air, so much fresher than that of Lisbon; there was shade in this little street, and no crowds, and soon he would be back at the Pensão, where he could change his damp clothes and have a bath and a cool drink. The distance did not, he thought, justify a taxi;

he had taken a few landmarks on his way to the station and he would enjoy the walk back. It had been a tiring, an exhausting afternoon, but he had accomplished his mission; in his wallet were three air tickets, three places on the next day's flight to London. This experience would, he thought, teach his family to stay at home where they belonged.

As he reached the wide main street, he met stronger breezes. From the head of a gentleman walking a little ahead of him rose a somewhat battered trilby hat which, after sailing through the air and rolling in the dust, came to rest at Mr. Channing's feet. He stooped, picked it up and handed it to its owner, and was not surprised to hear that the gruff words of thanks were spoken in English; nothing foreign, he had decided in the first glance, about this old chap. One of those small, wiry, fierce-looking, obviously British fellows you used to see commanding some of those old regiments.

'Thanks. This blasted wind,' said the earl.

For all his shortness of manner, he was in excellent humour. A man of simple tastes, he thought the standards at the Quinta de Narvão what he called overdone, but it had been kind of the Baronesa to invite them and it would be churlish to pick holes.

'A relief,' Mr. Channing said, 'after the heat of Lisbon.'

They were walking side by side, a very large

man and a very small one. The earl did not come up to Mr. Channing's shoulder, but nobody, after the first few moments, ever thought of him as a small man.

'Couldn't stick it m'self,' he said. 'That's why I came out to Sintra. You a resident or a visitor?'

'Oh, purely a visitor.'

'Can't see much to do here,' commented the earl.

'Good walks. Rather damp, I imagine, in winter.'

'You at an hotel?'

'No. We found a nice little Pen-sow; clean, and good value.'

The earl who understood and approved of good value, nodded.

'Best way to see a country,' he said. 'Well...'

He halted; the road to the Quinta lay to his right. He looked at Mr. Channing, placed him, liked him and made a gruff proposal.

'If you've time on your hands, we might do a walk or two,' he suggested. 'My plan is always to have a bit of breakfast and set off early; skip lunch and munch a few nuts, skip tea and come back to a good, solid dinner. That way, you can cover a lot of country without wasting time loading yourself up with food.'

This programme had no appeal whatsoever for Mr. Channing, and it was with relief that he remembered that he would be unable to fall in with it.

'As a matter of fact—' he began.

'Where can I find you?'

'Well, as I was about to tell you—'

'What's the name of that Pensow you mentioned?'

'The Pensão Pombal. But—'

'Whom shall I ask for?'

'My name's Channing, but—'

'I'm ...' The earl paused, his face growing slowly redder. 'Channing?' he repeated slowly. '*Channing?* You wouldn't by any chance be any ... No.' He answered himself. 'Pure coincidence.'

But Mr. Channing had once again—his wits sharpened, perhaps, by recent adversity—leapt to a correct conclusion: this little man whose manner was turning so rapidly from the friendly to the surprised to the suspicious to the snarling was James's grandfather. He was the Earl of Saxonford. He was the man who, without so much as a look at his grandson's choice of wife, had rejected her because she didn't have three million pounds in her pocket.

Anger, pride, paternal love and a general feeling that fate had overreached herself drove him to speak out with unwonted boldness.

'If you're wondering whether I'm any relation of the Channings your grandson knows—and I presume you're Lord Saxonford—let me tell you at once that I am Christine Channing's father.'

The two faced one another. They had

forgotten Sintra. They were no longer standing in a windy street in Portugal. The earl was in his study listening to his grandson raving about a girl he had picked up somewhere in London, and Mr. Channing was in his bedroom looking at his daughter sobbing in her mother's arms.

'You mean'—the earl began slowly to follow a horrifying train of thought—'you mean that you're *here*?'

'As you see,' said Mr. Channing.

'You're here, at Sintra, with your ... May I ask if your—'

'My wife and daughter are with me, yes,' Mr. Channing said stoutly. 'I have no need, I think, to tell you that we had no idea that you or your grandson would be anywhere near.'

The earl said nothing, but his expression spoke more plainly and more loudly than words, and Mr. Channing could read it clearly enough. Anger of a kind he seldom felt rose in him and made his hands shake.

'I should like your assurance,' he brought out with difficulty, 'that you accept my statement.'

'Pure coincidence, eh?' snarled the earl.

Something—a faint, scarcely-heard voice—told him that he had gone too far. Common sense, buried beneath rage, told him that his only quarrel was with a malevolent fate. But his temper was an inheritance that more than six hundred years had not sufficed to dilute. Long, long before his forebears had been earls,

181

they had been daring, dreaded Border chiefs who had led, not followed, Percys and Greys; who had harried and harassed Douglasses and Armstrongs and Eliots. Many an old Border ballad told of their fierce affrays—and their fierce tempers.

The latest-but-one descendant strove to rein in his fury. He had sauntered out—how long ago? surely only minutes?—from the wide terrace of the Quinta dos Castanheiros, glancing over his shoulder at a picture that had given him infinite pleasure: his grandson seated on a long chair beside his cousin Katherine, the two relaxed and at ease and content in one another's company. He had not, at that moment, dreamed that fate held any unpleasant surprises in store; he was convinced, on the contrary, that it was playing stoutly on his side. He had with the greatest difficulty persuaded his grandson to make the journey at all; he had been obliged, before leaving home, to agree to staying a bare week in Lisbon before driving home. But an unlooked-for check, a delay, an accident to the car—was that not clear proof of the benevolence of Providence?

And now to learn that this other girl and her parents were here, had fallen out of a blue sky at their very feet ... Was a man expected to smile and bow and express his pleasure, and call the whole thing coincidence?

His slowly clearing senses made him aware

that the large man confronting him had drawn out of his pocket a wallet. He was in fact brandishing it in his face.

'I have here,' Mr. Channing said slowly and clearly, 'three air tickets. I spent a hot, a tiring, a difficult afternoon in Lisbon trying to change our sea passages in order to get places on tomorrow's flight to London. I succeeded in changing the boat tickets. I managed, after much trouble, to get three places on tomorrow's plane. I was about to cut short our holiday and leave Portugal, and insist on my wife and my daughter's leaving Portugal, because I had learned, to my infinite dismay, that you and your grandson had arrived. We knew nothing of your movements; your presence here was as unwelcome to us as ours clearly is to you. Rather than risk any possibility of misunderstanding, I made up my mind to leave at once. But now'—he replaced the wallet in his pocket with an air of finality— 'nothing will induce me to leave. I shall stay here, and so will my wife and my daughter. Your movements, or your grandson's movements, do not interest me. Rest assured that I shall be as anxious, from now on, to keep my daughter away from your grandson as you are to keep him away from her. You do not deserve my daughter, and if I have anything to do with it, you won't get her. Good evening to you.'

Breathless, almost beside himself with rage,

he nevertheless retained calm enough to hope that he could remember every word of this speech, without alteration or omission, to repeat to his wife. He had not known himself capable of such force, such clarity. To think that all his life he had muttered, mumbled, faltered and fumbled, dropping frogs when he might have dropped pearls. Pride, together with a sense of having wasted a great gift, filled him. He had allowed his wife to speak for him, his daughters and his son to finish nine out of every ten sentences he uttered, while all the time he had been capable of this!

He turned on his heel; he wanted to get to his wife almost as much as he wanted to leave the earl. But he had taken only three steps when the earl's voice reached him.

'Stop!'

Mr. Channing stopped and turned.

'Well?'

'You have my apology. But you needn't trouble yourselves to go back to England,' the earl said curtly. 'My grandson and I will move to Lisbon until we are able to leave Portugal.'

Mr. Channing stared at him, and slowly an unholy joy filled him.

'You are,' he asked, 'at the Quinta de Narvão?'

'I am.'

'And you wish to leave?'

'I've just told you so.'

Mr. Channing gave a contemptuous smile.

The smile widened and became a soundless, shaking laugh. He tried to regain his sobriety, failed, and laughed aloud. Still laughing, he turned and went away.

He walked home with a firm, youthful stride. Turning into the courtyard of the Pensão Pombal, he saw his wife and daughter on the verandah. They came down the steps to meet him. Mrs. Channing, about to speak, looked at his expression and forgot what she was going to say.

'I got the air tickets,' Mr. Channing said in a firm, confident voice.

'Good,' said Christine. 'Then we—'

'For tomorrow,' went on her father.

'I packed, just in case,' said Mrs. Channing. 'Did—'

'But we are not going,' said Mr. Channing.

The two women stared at him.

'But—' began Christine.

'We are not going. We are staying here.'

'But I just told you,' Mrs. Channing said in a bewildered voice. 'You asked me to be ready, and so I packed.'

'Then you must unpack.'

Mrs. Channing looked at Christine. The two opened their lips to speak, glanced at Mr. Channing's red, resolute, unfamiliar face and closed them again. Mrs. Channing walked to the house and, followed by Maria-Jose, Maria-Helena and Maria-Innocencia, went upstairs to do the unpacking.

185

CHAPTER EIGHT

An hour later, James and Christine were seated together at the Café opposite the Palace, exchanging views on the situation.

'The trouble is,' James summed up at last, 'that my grandfather isn't really in his right mind.'

'My father's crazy too,' Christine said. 'To expect, to order me not to see you! That makes him even more feeble-minded than your grandfather. Your grandfather did at least have the sense to give up. What exactly happened when he got home?'

'Well, he came back from his walk looking as though a dog had bitten him. He'd gone out looking thoroughly happy, leaving Katie and myself looking—'

'Begin at the beginning. You agreed to part from me for three months. Next?'

'I settled down at home and waited to be thrown at Katie, or have Katie thrown at me. But my grandfather discovered that Katie and her mother were in London and wouldn't be up north for some time because they were going to Portugal. So he proposed taking off for Portugal too, which shook me, because it showed me for the first time to what lengths he was prepared to go to get his own way. He hates travelling; he hasn't left home for years.

To hear him actually proposing to come out to Portugal—'

'—shook you. Move on.'

'I told him that if we went, we'd go in my way; that is, not by train or air or boat, but in my car. I said I'd drive him out, stay in Katie's vicinity for one week and then drive him back by a different route. That way, we'd both enjoy ourselves. It was only a crumb, but he had to make do with crumbs, and so we set off. It was a good trip; I'll do it again with you for our honeymoon. That bit round about the Dordogne is—'

'Then you got here, and what?'

'We'd decided to stay in Lisbon. Katie and her mother met us at the hotel the evening we arrived and we asked them to come out to dinner. We were just deciding where to have it when someone turned up—a woman they'd met in England in connection with some dogs that Katie's mother had sold. Did I tell you she bred Great Danes?'

'No.'

'Well, she does. She sold a couple of them to a fellow in Portugal, and this Baronesa something-or-other went to England to collect them.'

'She brought them out on our boat.'

'She did? Well, if that isn't a—'

'—coincidence; quite. If I have to work as hard to keep you on the rails morally as I'm doing conversationally, I'm going to lead a

187

busy life.'

'Where did I leave off?'

'You were about to dine with your grandfather, with Katie and her mother and with the Baronesa Narvão.'

'The Baronesa had asked Katie's mother to stay with her when she came out to Portugal, but Katie'd already fixed up with some French friends of hers at this Quinta dos Castanheiros. The Baronesa dropped in to see them on the morning of our arrival, heard we were on our way out and said she'd like to meet us. That was why she turned up at the hotel—she said she happened to be passing. She very kindly offered to put us up at her house, but we refused, naturally, because we didn't even know her. She stayed rather a long time, so in the end we asked her to join us for dinner. I wanted to leave my car at a garage overnight for servicing, so she offered to lead me to one she knew. The others went in her car and I drove behind as far as the garage; I left the car there, told them what I wanted and arranged to call for it in the morning. Then I joined the others in the Baronesa's car and her chauffeur drove us to a restaurant. On the way, my grandfather learned that her house was a mere stone's throw from the place that Katie and her mother were staying at, so—'

'—so he wished he'd said yes in the first place. Go on.'

'Next morning, I went along to get my car.

188

They told me it was ready. I paid the bill and I was just walking across the yard to get to it, when out of nowhere came a damned great truck. It went straight towards my car and I stood watching it thinking the driver was off his rocker, but feeling quite certain he'd pull the truck round in time. But he didn't. He hit the car with a crash you could have heard all the way to Sintra, wrecked one of the mudguards and buckled a wheel—and then drove straight out on to the road and vanished. I couldn't believe I'd seen what I'd seen— because what I'd seen, I realized after a moment or two, wasn't a truck out of control but a deliberate attempt to wreck my car.'

'Did you get the truck's number?'

'No. The whole thing happened too quickly. I went back and told my grandfather we were stuck, and he said that in that case, he'd avail himself of the Baronesa's hospitality. I said no, we wouldn't. I'd only just finished saying it when a message came from below to say the Baronesa would like to see us. We went down, and she told us she'd heard our car had packed up.'

'And she wouldn't go away until you and your grandfather had packed up and accompanied her back to the Quinta de Narvão.'

'Yes. After a lifetime of telling me never to talk to strangers, my grandfather decided to stay with one. As far as comfort goes, we couldn't have fallen on softer ground, but I can't help feeling that there's something about the whole thing that's—'

'And then your grandfather met my father and—'

'I wish,' James said longingly, 'I could have seen that meeting.'

'My father said your grandfather insulted him grossly and practically accused us of racing out here to lay ourselves in your path. So he told him what he thought of him—and of you. He recited the whole speech to mother and then, in case she'd missed any of it, he ran through it again. And again. And then he told me that you were the grandson of a raving lunatic, not to say an out-of-date and arrogant old humbug, and ordered me never to think of you again. And just after he'd got all that out, Gustavo—the owner of the Pensão—came in with your note.'

'I got as far as a phone and then thought better of it. You might have refused to come to the phone, but I thought you'd read a letter if I sent one.'

'Well, I read it. And here I am. You lured me out by promising me dinner. When's dinner?'

'Presently.' James signalled a waiter and ordered more drinks. 'What I want to know first is why your father laughed when my grandfather spoke of leaving the Quinta de Narvão.'

Christine hesitated.

'It's a long story,' she said at last.

'We shall dine,' James said, 'when you've told me.'

She told him.

At the end of her recital, he sat staring at the table, saying nothing. She waited for his comments, but they were so long in coming that she added an appendix.

'You're probably thinking,' she said, 'that just because your grandfather's an earl, she'll have him—and you—for free. I'm absolutely certain that tomorrow, or the day after, he'll be handed his bill. What will he do?'

James considered.

'He'll tear it up before her eyes, and dance on the pieces,' he said at last.

'He can dance right through the hornpipe, but he'll still have to pay. Has she or hasn't she got your passports?'

'That's nothing to go by; she'd have to ask for them; it's the law.'

'Try to get them back.'

'There must,' James said slowly, 'be a hitch somewhere. If she's what you say she is, she's a crook.'

'Don't be unkind. Let's just say she's a swindling shark.'

'Crook or shark,' James declared with conviction, 'nobody can do a thing like this to my grandfather and get away with it.'

'Until she sees the colour of your money, you're stuck. Go ahead and try to get away

191

without paying. It's easy—just so long as you don't need your passports.'

'But ... you and your parents got out without paying the full amount.'

'Only because...'

She pulled herself up sharply. They had got out because the Baronesa wanted to get James and his grandfather in. That was the simple fact, and there was no need to complicate it by imagining there could be any possible connection between the talk that she and Gustavo and Felipe had had on the verandah, and James's arrival at the Quinta de Narvão with his grandfather.

'We were lucky, that's all,' she ended lamely.

He looked at her closely.

'That isn't what you were going to say. You began something and then pulled yourself up. What was it?'

'Nothing.'

'It was ... You don't, by any chance, know something about this business that you haven't told me?'

Help came from an unexpected quarter. A car passed them, its progress so erratic that James turned to look at it in astonishment.

'Did you see that?' he asked. 'Fancy allowing an old crone like that to drive a car. She ought to be in a bath-chair. If I were the chap sitting beside her, I'd ... Good Lord! It's Charles Granger! Who on earth is that apparition with him?'

'His aunt,' Christine said unwarily, and saw James looking at her in surprise.

'You knew he was here?'

'Yes.'

'Does he know you're here?'

'Yes, he does.'

'You wouldn't have let him know,' James said, 'that you were coming out to Portugal?'

'Oh, for goodness sake! He came out here to stay with his apparition of an aunt. Now can I have dinner?'

They were halfway through their meal when the door of the restaurant opened and Charles appeared.

'Hoped you'd be here,' he said, coming up to their table. 'Can I join you?'

'Where's your aunt?' James asked apprehensively.

'At home. I saw you and Christine near the Palace and came out to see if I could locate you. I didn't really believe that story Christine told me about staying away from you for three months. Where're you staying, James?'

James looked at Christine.

'You tell him,' he said.

Christine told him, and the menu dropped from Charles's nerveless hand.

'*No!*' he exclaimed, aghast.

'Yes,' said James. 'Me and my grandfather, both. I don't want any comments from you; Christine's said it all.'

Charles ordered his meal, and as they ate,

they agreed that while Charles would be unwelcome as a third on sight-seeing expeditions, as a fourth he would make a good partner for Katherine.

'Transport's a difficulty,' James pointed out. 'There's no hope of getting my car yet.'

'I could get my aunt's,' said Charles, 'but she'd be in it.'

'In that case, I'll hire one,' said James. 'Let's all meet tomorrow at that Pombal place. Ten-thirty?'

'Suits me,' said Charles. 'Will you bring your cousin?'

'Yes. You'll like her.'

'I'll have to,' Charles said. 'I've got a fat chance of seeing any more of Christine.'

'What's she like?' Christine asked James.

'What's who like?'

'Your cousin Katherine. Describe her.'

James waved a hand vaguely.

'Oh ... fair hair, quite reasonable-looking, brainy; did brilliantly at Oxford. Sort of serious, I'd say.'

With this unfinished portrait Christine had to be content until she saw the original stepping out of James's hired car at the Pensão Pombal next morning. Katherine Staples proved to be rather small, slim, with a pretty figure, smooth fair hair, a small nose and a large, well-shaped mouth. Her eyes were blue, her manner somewhat detached; she sat listening to the conversation as though she did not expect to participate in it. Mr. and Mrs. Channing, passing through the verandah on their way out for a walk, stopped for a few words and received the impression that James's cousin was a nice girl but that Christine, on the whole, had nothing to fear.

Mr. Channing had a brief exchange with James.

'Christine told you about our experience at the Baronesa's.'

'Yes, sir.'

'Did you tell your grandfather?'

'Yes, I did.'

'And I suppose he didn't believe a word?'

'He did his best not to believe it—but it put him on his guard. He told the Baronesa this morning that he's planning a short trip into Spain. He isn't, but it'll be a sort of try out. He told her that the trip was to take place three days from now; if she doesn't lay our passports on his plate on the third day, he'll know where he is.'

'He'll know what she is. Be interesting to know what she charges you. I'd like to know whether she's got a fixed scale, or whether she puts on twenty per cent for peers.'

'I'll tell you, sir—if we get a bill.'

'You'll get a bill,' Mr. Channing promised him.

'I'd like to know,' he remarked to his wife as they set off for their walk, 'what that old fellow thinks about his grandson hobnobbing round the Pensão all day.'

'I dare say he spoke as severely to him as you did to Christine,' said his wife placidly. 'And with equal success.'

'Serves him right for trying to interfere. I could have told him to keep out of young people's affairs. Did you ever see me interfering when the house was full of all those young men of Barbara's and Antoinette's?'

Mrs. Channing was able to say, with truth, that he had shown an admirable detachment.

'Well, I'll show it now,' promised Mr. Channing. 'We've as much right to visit Portugal as anybody else, and if people want their grandsons to keep away from a girl, that's their business. That cousin of James,' he added, 'is going to feel a bit out of it. Three's a crowd.'

'Four. I saw Charles Granger coming down the lane.'

Charles arrived to find that, as he had suspected, the party was not a foursome, but two twosomes. Seated at a table on the verandah sketching out a rough programme, it became clear that James was going to drive, Christine was going to sit beside him and if the other two cared to occupy the back seats, well and good.

There was a sharp difference of opinion about sight-seeing. James declared himself willing to look at any sights that could be fitted in on the way to a beach. Charles agreed with this, but the two girls protested.

'What's the use of being out here and only seeing beaches?' asked Christine.

'We can bathe at home,' pointed out Katherine in her quiet, somewhat precise voice. 'I've always been interested in Portugal, and there's a lot I'd like to see. It's got such an interesting history; in fact, the history of the Peninsula as a whole is fascinating. I was trying to remember which Alfonso it was whose daughter married Henry of Burgundy and was given the north of Portugal as a dowry. He had six wives, but no sons.'

'Tough,' muttered Charles, staring at her in awe. Mixed with awe was apprehension. Big brain, big strain; he hoped he would not be called upon to keep up with anything too erudite.

'Teresa—that was her name,' said Katherine. 'She had a son called Alfonso Henriques. It was he, I think, who first made Portugal recognized as a separate kingdom—in 1143, wasn't it?'

'As near as makes no matter,' said Charles.

'I vote we find this Estoril beach and spread ourselves out,' said James. 'Everybody here is dark brown, and my white torso shames me. How about food, Christine? Can your landlord give us a cold lunch to take with us?'

Gustavo fetched his wife, who went inside again to prepare a picnic. They were given two large baskets, a striped blanket to sit on, a huge black umbrella to sit under, and a *garafao* of red wine. The whole family assembled to see them off.

'I ought to go and tell my aunt I won't be back to lunch,' Charles said as they drove down the lane.

'When you don't turn up, she'll know you're not there,' said James. 'What's the sea temperature here?'

'Zero,' said Charles. 'You others can swim if you like, but not me. I'll sunbathe.'

He lay on the beach watching the others enter the water with varying degrees of fortitude. Christine and James swam over and boarded one of the bicycle floats and pedalled their way out to sea again; Katherine came to sit beside Charles, her skin wet and glistening in the warm sunshine.

'Was it cold?' Charles asked, squinting up at her from under the arm flung across his eyes.

'It was nice. The beach looked very pretty when I was swimming. There are some lovely flowers up on those banks over there.'

He sat up and handed her a small wooden backrest and she propped herself against it and spoke thoughtfully.

'Isn't it fascinating to think that flowers were dedicated to heathen gods, and to saints? The maidenhair to Pluto, the narcissus to Ceres, the vine of course to Bacchus. What were the others?'

Charles looked apprehensively out to sea;

198

those floats, he remembered, were hired by the hour.

'Well, let me see,' he said, frowning. 'The maidenhair to Pluto, I think it was; the vine to ... Oh, you said that. The narcissus to Ceres; interesting, when you come to think of it.'

'And the saints. The daisy to St. Margaret and the crocus to St. Valentine and St. Barnabas's thistle to—'

'—St. Barnabas.'

'Yes. So few people seem to know, but it's so fascinating. Think of all the funeral plants: laurel, cypress, amaranth and—'

'Speaking of laurel, the Greeks used to—'

'Laurel wreaths to the victor in the Pythian games?'

'Eh? Oh yes, yes. I knew a pair of twins once who were called Laurel and Camilla. One married—'

'Camilla ... A virgin queen of the Volscians—wasn't that the Roman legend?'

'Well, this Camilla I was talking about—'

'Virgil said she was so swift that she could run over a field of corn without bending a single blade. She could go over the sea without wetting her feet.'

'Like the Hovercraft. You—'

'What were those lines? The ones that begin:

"Not so when swift Camilla scours the plain."

Can you remember?'

199

'I'm afraid I can't.' Charles wished that he could go as swiftly as Camilla, leaving Katherine behind. Disappointment filled him; there had been something about this girl, he told himself, that he had liked. You had to admit that life was always springing surprises; here he was on a warm beach with a girl, and all he could get her to talk about was Camilla scouring the plain. It wasn't, you could tell, an act; the girl was simply being natural. Under that wet hair was a vast accumulation of knowledge, most of it the sort of thing sensible people forgot when they left school, if they ever knew it.

'Do you like dancing?' he asked. After all, she must have some human pleasures.

'I'm not awfully good at ballroom, but I once did ballet. And once, when I was at school in France, we did a *dance champêtre* and all wore oak leaves and garlands and loathed it. I once saw a rather good attempt at the Salic dances—you know, instituted by Numa Pompilius ... *was* it Numa Pompilius?'

'Very likely.'

'In honour of Mars.'

'Sounds like a sort of Roman mothers' day,' said Charles recklessly. 'What did they do, exactly?'

'Twelve priests were chosen from the nobility, and they danced in the temple while sacrifices were being made.'

'Gory, I call it.'

'But perhaps it wasn't Numa Pompilius. Don't you know?'

'Frankly, I don't. Let's come to grips with it: I don't know much about anything. I was up at Oxford until the authorities got to hear of it, and then they asked me to go away and make room for more promising material. All I know anything about, to tell you the shameful truth, is cricket and racing.'

'Racing? What sort of racing?'

'What sort of ... Well, I don't mean the four-minute mile or trotting or free-style or rounding the buoy. When I say racing, I mean Ascot and Epsom and Aintree.'

'I like that kind of racing, too. I never miss a Derby.'

'First time I ever went was with an aunt—this peculiar aunt of mine who lives here. She goes back to Spion Kop and Humorist and Captain Cuttle—fantastic.'

'What were they—Derby winners?'

'Of course. Isn't that what we were talking about?' He sat up and looked at her more attentively. 'Do you like cricket too?'

'I love cricket. Isn't it odd that hardly anybody knows why Lord's is called Lord's? It was Thomas Lord, a groundsman, who—'

'No, really? I once,' Charles said in a reverent tone, 'met Don Bradman. He came to Speech Day and autographed my bat. I was quite a decent batsman, but you don't get much time once you've got your nose down to the grindstone. My grandfather was at that varsity match in 1870.'

'Which one?'

'*The* one. D'you mean to say you've never read Lyttleton?'

'Never.'

'Well, quite frankly, you ought to get your mind off those temple dancers and concentrate on essentials. That finish in 1870 made cricket history.'

Katherine studied him.

'You mentioned a grindstone. What do you work at?'

'I sell cars. I sell expensive cars, which is easy. Selling cheap cars is harder, because obviously you're selling to people who have to worry about hanging on to their money.'

She kept her mild blue eyes on him.

'You're in love with Christine, aren't you?' she asked calmly.

'Well ... yes and no.'

'Can you be indefinite about a thing like that?'

'I can. You wouldn't understand; you've got a good brain and your thinking is obviously along more elevated lines than mine. All I ever think about is cricket, racing, show-jumping, skiing—and girls. Roughly in that order. I'm a good cricketer, I go racing in the cheap stands, I watch show-jumping on television and I ski when my birthday cheques add up to a total large enough to allow it. I'm lucky; my birthday's in January, so I can go in February and get the best snow. How did I get on to skiing?'

'You were wondering whether you were, or weren't in love with Christine.'

'At the moment, I'm not. I fell in love with her and then had to put in time while she went off with James, and there was a girl at Soissons it was easy to put in time with. People like you can't understand chaps like myself; I've so little in my head that once the cricket season's over, and in between racing and skiing, I'm left in the air.'

'You're pretending to be stupid, but you're not.'

'Nobody ever said I was stupid. I'm just trying to get across to you the fact that I can't sustain any conversation above the cricket-racing-girl level.'

'I can talk about racing. I've got a system.'

'A what?'

'A system.'

'You *have*?'

'Yes.'

'Tell me.'

'I invented it myself. It's a little complicated. You may perhaps...'

'Wait till I get out my pen and a bit of paper. Now, expound.'

She was still expounding when James and Christine joined them and set about opening the picnic baskets. She expounded as they ate, and after they had eaten. She and Charles, engrossed, elected to remain on the beach for the afternoon, and hardly noticed the departure of James and Christine.

'They'll find their own way back,' James said as he carried the baskets to the car. 'Where would you like to go?'

'Across the river.'

On the warm hills above Arrábida, they lay and talked of themselves and of their future. James fell asleep and Christine kept watch over him, brushing off flies and gazing at him with tenderness and wondering whether they would be faithful all their lives, as her father and mother had been faithful.

Only when they were on their way home did James remember matters that had slipped to the back of his mind.

'I've been thinking about that truck episode,' he told Christine. 'One or two details have been coming back to me.'

'Such as?'

'It was a green truck. That doesn't take us far—but I remember seeing some splashes of red paint on the side. And I remember something else, too: the driver's face. I can't tell you whether he was a small chap or a big one, but he had a Chinese-type face, as a lot of these Portuguese do. He was young, and he had on a black peaked cap. If I ever saw him again, I'd know him—and if I ever do see him again, I'll bash him, as he bashed my car. The more I think of it, the more I'm convinced it was no accident. It was a deliberate and, I must say, beautifully executed manoeuvre. I went along to the garage and described him and told them to keep an eye out for him. I'm doing the same myself.'

Christine, walking slowly up the verandah steps when he had left her, sat on one of the little chairs to think the matter out. Felipe had asked for a night's delay. Felipe was young. Felipe had a Chinese-type face and wore a black peaked cap. But to imagine Felipe in a green truck bearing down upon James's car ...

Felipe would be here later this evening, to visit Maria de Fatima. There would be no harm in asking him a few questions.

It was some time before she could get him alone. When her parents went to bed, she stayed on the verandah with the family, but it was almost midnight before Felipe left Maria de Fatima and came to sit on the steps close to Christine's chair.

'Your father and mother—the Senhor and the Senhora—do not like to stay late?' he asked her.

'They were tired. Do you have to go back to Lisbon tonight?' she asked in her turn.

'Oh, no, no! I live in Sintra, very close.'

'But you work in Lisbon?'

'Yes. I work in a garage.'

'Then that,' Christine said, 'explains everything.'

He gave her an upward, wary glance.

'Please?'

'You were driving a green truck.'

He watched her expression for a few moments, but the verandah light was too dim for him to know what she was thinking.

'You hear about truck?'

'You hit a car—deliberately. Purposely. Do you know whose car it was? It was my fiancé's.'

He twisted round to stare up at her.

'Your *noivo!*'

'No less. Now you can tell me why you damaged his car.'

'You are angry?'

'He's angry. He's looking for you.'

'He has the number?'

'No. But he remembers what you look like, and when he sees you ...'

'I did not know he was your *noivo*. You are going to tell him about me?'

'No. I can't bear the sight of blood.'

She saw his sudden, wicked grin. She smiled back—unwisely, she thought; it established them as allies in a plot to which as yet she had no key.

'Will you please tell me,' she asked, 'why you did it?'

His English, good enough for short exchanges, broke down under the strain of a consecutive account. She had to supply words, disentangle grammar and clarify mistakes. But in the end the story emerged—without a moral, but with an interlocking of detail which made her feel that fate had indeed stretched out a hand.

Felipe, in the course of his duties, had driven to the Quinta dos Castanheiros to deliver a car which had been serviced at the garage in which he worked. While he was there, the Baronesa had called; chatting with her chauffeur and one or two of the maids, Felipe had learned, without much interest, that an English lord and his grandson were expected in Lisbon that evening. He had then, inevitably, made his way to the Pensão Pombal in the hope of seeing Maria de Fatima and getting some lunch. He had been put to wood-chopping, and then his labours were interrupted so that he could act as interpreter. He had learned that Christine and her family were in the clutches of the Baronesa and hoped to come back to the Pensão Pombal—and he remembered, suddenly, that an English lord was to arrive, and that the Baronesa would obviously learn of his impending arrival. His proposition to Gustavo was simple enough: when he went back to Lisbon, he would try to find out where the lord was staying; he was arriving by car, and who knew? Perhaps a man who understood about cars could make a little adjustment and cause a little delay—and after that? After that it would only be necessary to inform the Baronesa that the lord's car was damaged; the Baronesa could be relied upon to do the rest.

But the saints, Felipe asserted at this point, were on his side. Who, that evening, should come to the garage? To the very garage, the garage in which he worked? The Baronesa, followed by the grandson of the lord. The car was left at the garage, to be called for on the following morning. Could that be coincidence? It was nonsense to say so. All that remained was to wait until the next day—and to have the truck ready. That way, no blame would attach to the garage; could they help it if a madman came suddenly and made a collision? A happy memory brought back the grin to Felipe's face, and he dashed his two fists together.

'Poombah!' he said. 'It made a loud noise.'

Christine sat silent, fitting the pieces together. The Baronesa had failed to induce Katherine Staples and her mother to stay with her. Visiting them, she had learned of the imminent arrival of two of their friends. Passing the hotel—quite by chance, she said— she met James and his grandfather and was invited to dine with them. James had driven to the garage in the wake of the Baronesa, thus establishing the link; the rest could be left to Felipe.

'He remembers,' she said at last, 'the red paint on the side of the truck.'

'Paint? No, not paint,' Felipe said. 'Paper. There was an ad ... adver ...'

'Advertisement?'

'Yes. I took him—took it off. Cleaned off.

But all is now good, no? Car no good, *noivo*
stay.'

'How do you think he likes staying at the
Baronesa's?'

Felipe's shoulders came up in the gesture
that said so much.

'It is a pity—but for you, he will be glad to be
there, no?'

'No,' said Christine. She rose to say good
night and he got to his feet and stood smilingly
before her. 'If my *noivo* ever sees you...'

He sketched a knockout blow on his chin.

'Poombah!'

'Quite,' said Christine.

CHAPTER NINE

Mrs. Channing, seated on the verandah with
her husband two days later, watched absently a
shadow, or a shape that came and went in a
dark patch of woodland beyond the house.

'Dreaming?' her husband enquired.

'No. I just thought I saw someone dodging
about in those trees.'

'Robin Hood,' said Mr. Channing, with
unwonted facetiousness.

He was feeling very cheerful. The trip to
Portugal, disastrous at the outset, was proving,
after all, a success. The humiliation he had
endured at the Baronesa's hands had less sting

now that he could be certain the earl was soon to undergo it. He could look back upon his encounter with the old man with satisfaction and pride, knowing that he had more than held his own. He liked Sintra, not less for the clouds which frequently obscured the sun and brought a welcome coolness. He could, and did, say *Bom dia, boa noite, faz favor* and *obrigado*, feeling as he did so that nobody could ever again accuse him of insularity. He slept reasonably well in spite of the nightly noises. He ate a very good breakfast, digested it—as now—on the verandah, and precisely at 11 o'clock went for a walk. This took the form of a pleasant stroll and had no relation to the marathon proposed by the earl—more suited, he thought, to jockeys intent on losing weight than to elderly men of uncertain temper. The walk ended at the café opposite the Palace, where the Colonel usually came to meet them. The beer was cheap and good and it was interesting to watch the bus-loads of tourists disembarking and streaming up the steps of the Palace.

He rose and put on the hat bought the day before under the Colonel's advice and guidance; it was a compromise between a Panama and a deer-stalker, and made him feel very travelled.

'See you in the Square,' he said to Mrs. Channing.

She nodded, and watched him set off, his

departure punctuated by stops to pat the little girls, wave to the girls at the tank or have a word or two with Gustavo. She thought he looked well, but she looked forward with some dread to the moment when he mounted the bathroom scales on his return home. In the meantime, she was enjoying herself, happy because he was happy and Christine reunited with James.

Her eyes went back to the puzzling movements in the wood. The shadow was deep, but she was certain that she had seen a figure dart out from behind a tree, and dart back again. Yes ... there it was. Probably a workman of sorts. But surely...

The figure emerged into dappled sunlight and began to move in the direction of the house. As it came nearer, amazed speculation sprang into her mind and soon turned to certainty. The small, spare, upright figure now marching firmly towards her was—it couldn't be—but it must be James's grandfather. She rose and went to stand by the railing. He came on unhesitatingly, clambered with agility over the low wall, walked across the courtyard and up the steps and, coming to a halt beside her, raised his ancient trilby hat.

'Mrs. Channing?'

'James's grandfather,' she said. 'But you were ... surely you weren't hiding!'

'I certainly was.' He spoke gruffly, brusquely. 'Mind if we sit down?'

Mrs. Channing led him to a table, and they sat down and studied one another across it.

'You weren't hiding, surely,' she asked, 'from my husband?'

'I most certainly was.' The earl placed his hat carefully on the table in front of him. 'If he'd been a reasonable man, I would have made an attempt to put my point of view before him— but he's not a reasonable man. A fellow of that kind, who goes off at half-cock before a man's had time to open his mouth and say a few words, isn't a fellow you can hope to engage in reasonable discussion. So I took a look at you there at that café in the Square and I told m'self that you looked a woman of sense, and I came along here today and hung about until he'd gone off for what he calls a walk, in the hope of getting a word or two with you alone. Walk! It wouldn't even shake the mosquitoes off his trouser legs. Man of that size, I would have said, needed to tone up his liver. Come to think of it, that's obviously what's the matter with him. He ought to watch that temper of his.'

'Perhaps your temper could do with a bit of watching too,' suggested Mrs. Channing mildly.

'That's different. I'm quiet enough until I'm provoked. Your husband doesn't need provocation. Did he pause to look at this matter from my point of view? Not a bit of it. He launched into a spate of abuse and then walked off.'

'If he hadn't seen your point of view, would he have agreed to your separating your grandson and my daughter for three months while you tried to persuade James to change his mind?'

'Now *that*,' said the earl violently, 'was a namby-pamby way of going on, for a start.' He lifted his hat a few inches and brought it down again with a force that rattled the table. 'When James came back and told me that there you were, you and your husband, sitting down to watch your daughter mumble and mope for three months, I said to m'self: Soft lot. If I'd had a daughter, I said to m'self, I'd like to see the grandfather who tried to put a spoke in her wheel. I'd have broken his head, and then broken his grandson's head for giving in. What sent your husband off the handle the other day when we met? The feeling that I thought he'd trailed his daughter across James's path. Well, and if he had, I would have thought him—after a moment or two, if he'd waited—a better man. Dammit, didn't I say over and over again that I had nothing against your daughter? From what I'd heard and from what I've seen, she's a pretty, well-behaved girl and I've no doubt she'll make a good enough wife—but she won't bring any money with her, and what is there left to be mistress of? Without money, most of the land'll have to go. What does that leave? A crumbling castle that the National Trust may or may not take over, and a few thousand acres. The place has been running downhill for the last hundred years. If James doesn't marry a woman who'll bring in some money to buttress it up, he'll find himself left with nothing but an old title and some old battle trophies. And there'—picking up his hat, he banged it down again in a way that made Mrs. Channing understand why it looked so battered—'there you have it.'

He paused for breath and Mrs. Channing prepared to say one or two of the things that had occurred to her in the course of his monologue. But the earl had by no means finished.

'Dare say you find it hard,' he went on, 'to see my side of it. Dare say you feel that your daughter's happiness matters more than a crumbling castle. I wouldn't be surprised if you were even of the opinion that owners of estates they can't keep up any longer ought to put on their glasses and read the writing on the wall. You might even go as far as to say that the land I'm so anxious to keep was filched, in the first place, from somebody else. You might go a bit further and recall that we owe the title to a whore of a waiting-maid. I give you all that— but what you rob, you fight to keep. What you acquire, by whatever means, you're not too anxious to give away again. We're a family of fighters—we sprang, if you like, from robbers, but in those old days you fought for what you wanted. Lately, we've fought a losing battle to

214

keep what we won, and I don't relish seeing my grandson throwing away the last chance of hanging on to our possessions.'

'I suppose not,' agreed Mrs. Channing. 'But—'

''Tisn't as though Katie hadn't been a nice girl. You've seen her—what could a young man have against her? But your daughter came along, and my attempts to interfere came to nothing but a hash.'

'I'm sorry that—'

'Our trouble,' said the earl morosely, 'is that we never were collectors. We never went in for pictures or plate. We started off as a rough lot and we remained a rough lot. If we'd been more civilized—more cultured, if you like—we would have filled the place with stuff that would fetch high prices today. But we didn't. All we had to sell was land, and more land and more land and ... Good God! there was his cousin Katherine with a fortune and a good, strong, healthy girl into the bargain!'

'The bargain,' repeated Mrs. Channing thoughtfully.

'If you like, yes. The bargain.' The earl looked fiercely across the table and then turned aside to glare at Gustavo, who had come up to them. 'What's this fellow want?'

'He wants to offer you something to drink.'

'Well, tell him to go away.'

'I,' said Mrs. Channing coldly, 'would like some coffee.'

215

'Oh. Well, that's different,' conceded the earl. 'Sorry. No, not for me; never take it. Poison, if you ask me. Rot-gut. What was I saying?'

'You were wondering why James hadn't fallen in love with his cousin.'

'Well, I do wonder. James thinks just as much of the place as I do and as his father did. I myself saw the end coming, and I put aside my own feelings and married a girl who could bring in something. But she didn't, in the end. Her father gambled it all away before we could lay our hands on a penny of it. James's father went his own way and married a girl with a few paltry thousands that got swallowed up before you could look round; she used it for damnfool things like heating and bathrooms. I've nothing against warmth and cleanliness, but you can be warm and clean and still starve. While you're having your bath, prices are rising, values are falling, tenants are screeching for repairs, your creditors are dunning you and ... Well, what's the use of talking? James'll travel his own road and I shan't be here, thank God, to see the end of it. We'll finish up as we began—with a few acres and a host of dependents. But there'll be no replenishing, no snatching, no grabbing the other fellow's land or cattle or even women. No. We got where we got by fighting, but you can't fight your own battles any more, more's the pity. I would have said all this to your husband if he'd been a reasonable man, but when those big fellows run amok, you're wise to keep out of their way. I'd be no match for him, even if I could knock thirty years off my age. In our family, we run small-small, big-big; my son was my size, but James and his sons will be outsize. And then the next two generations will be small again. You'll see.'

'I'm afraid I won't.'

'No, I suppose not. Well, that's got one thing off my mind. There's something else. This business of the Baronesa. James said that she had invited you and then handed in a stiff list of charges. That's what I came to talk about. There must be something about the story that he misunderstood. She's a rich woman with a house full of treasures. In fact, I'm sick of looking at the treasures; she's got a bracelet festooned with keys and she unlocks all the cabinets and tells you what each piece in the collection cost.'

'And which king, queen or prince or princess gave it to her, but she will not say which.'

'You went through it too, did you? If you ask me, that stuff is what she's collected from her victims in lieu of cash. She's got a collection there worth a mint. She can't be short of money.'

'But she is. She wants to keep her treasures and her house and her style of living. She wants to keep her army of servants, her magnificent table, her warmth and her comfort and her ease. She's watched her friends selling off their possessions one by one until they've no more to sell, and she's determined to keep what she's got, and also to put aside enough for a luxurious old age. I don't think she has any private income at all—but so long as she can keep the house full of guests and make them pay, she can meet her bills. I didn't understand this fully until she talked to me on the terrace one afternoon. Colonel Bell-Burton—a friend of my husband's, who lives here—told us the truth about her when he discovered we'd been presented with a bill, but I didn't really see the whole picture until the Baronesa gave me her own point of view.'

The earl sat considering for some time.

'Must be some way,' he said, 'to get the better of her. If she's well known, how does it come about that she can go on and on cheating people.'

'She doesn't exactly cheat. As the Colonel pointed out to us, she gives you something for your money. If you're wondering whether perhaps we mistook her invitation, I can assure you that when she heard we were staying here, she insisted on our being her guests. I can't remember her exact words, but nothing could have been clearer than her attitude: she professed to like us and to want us to stay with her as friends. My husband had seen something of her on the way out from England. My daughter and I hadn't; we were seasick and

218

in our cabins all the way to Lisbon, but my husband isn't a man to accept hospitality from strangers except under very warm pressure. We didn't stay long. He went to her to say that we were leaving—'

'—and got handed the bill. Well, she needn't try it with me.'

'It needn't happen to you. I don't suppose she made out bills for all those kings and queens.'

'I'll tell you something,' the earl said. 'I've got robber blood in my veins, and I dare say it goes back longer, and runs stronger than hers. My forebears didn't take kindly to extortion, and I'm not going to let her mistake me for another sitting bird.'

'You can't fly far without your passport.'

'I've asked for 'em. Said I was going into Spain. She said they were with the police and I said well that was all right, just to tell the police to have 'em back in time for me to go to Spain. If not, I shall go to the police myself and demand 'em.'

'I don't think you will. She'll explain that the police returned them and she unfortunately mislaid them. I don't want to depress you, but if she really is going to give you a bill, I don't think you'll get your passports until you've paid it.'

'I could tell the police she's holding up our passports. If she insisted she'd lost them, I suppose we could arrange to get new ones through the Consulate in Lisbon? The police, after all, must know all about her.'

'What is there to know? She lures gullible strangers into her house on the pretence of giving them free hospitality and then charges them for it. To me, it seems that her real genius lies in the kind of people she chooses—people who might protest, who might even protest violently, but who are only too anxious to get out of a situation which reflects very little credit on their social sense or on their sagacity. Neither you nor my husband, in the normal way, would dream of entering a stranger's house and accepting hospitality on such a scale. But you, like ourselves and like all those others before us, were foreigners, and in slight difficulties, and we could all persuade ourselves that perhaps she was eccentric, or lonely, or that she didn't have the same code of behaviour as ourselves and liked having us. We accept, and we get an outrageous bill and we suddenly see ourselves for the naïve fools that we are. It isn't a picture we really want to publicize—and so we don't go to too great lengths to fight the Baronesa.'

The earl sat silent for some time, his fierce expression giving way to a look of gloom. Her words, Mrs. Channing felt, must have cooled his warrior's blood; they had certainly given him food for thought. She waited for him to digest the full and unpalatable meal, taking in meanwhile the details of his small, spare figure

220

and strong, dark face with its prominent nose and brooding eyes. She tried to find a word that summed him up, and came to the conclusion that nothing short of formidable would do. It was an odd term to apply to an elderly gentleman seated on a sunny verandah between the roses that cascaded from the railing and the pink geraniums that spilled from the brightly painted pots, but she felt strongly that his grey flannel trousers, his neat jacket, the battered hat on the table in front of him, were all part of an unsuitably chosen fancy dress. He looked what he was: a fighter. His attitude was one of ease, but she did not think that he looked relaxed; he had an at-the-ready air that reminded her of the long, lean cats slinking about the courtyard, eating what they could find with one eye on the food and the other on the look-out for enemies, seeming, even when curled up asleep in a sunny corner of the stables, to have left something of themselves on guard, ready to spring into defensive or offensive action.

She saw her visitor rising to his feet.

'I suppose you're going along to meet your husband?' he asked.

'Yes.'

'Then, with your permission, I'll go along with you as far as the Square.'

They walked up the lane together, and on the way the earl gave Mrs. Channing his views on life.

'Glad I'm leaving it soon,' he told her. 'Glad I'm not bringing children into it any more. You can have it. I've lived to see everything I believed in as a boy torn up and thrown to the four winds. All we're good for now is sitting chewing sandwiches in front of a television set. The whole nation will sit, today, watching a fine play or a splendid opera, and see it broken into while they're told to go and clean their teeth with some goddam paste or other. Is that conditioning, or isn't it? If men and women of good brain and background and education have been made to swallow that without kicking the advertisers right through the picture and out the other side, what does that make them? But I don't suppose you agree with me.'

'I do. So would my husband.'

'But neither of you have ever made any form of protest?'

'No.'

'Well, I have. You can keep it, I said to them. You can take the set right back to wherever it came from. It's not for me. Radio was all right; you could listen and get on with whatever you were doing. I used to leave a portable set running in the kitchen garden, to scare the birds. You can have television. You can have it all, in fact. All we're good for now is waiting to be told what to do next. What to think next. Am I right?'

'Well, I—'

'Of course I am. Take those so-called teenagers. There they are, youngsters at a stage of development at which you could teach 'em anything; anything. You could train them, lead them into something—and where do they go? Into the nearest gramophone shop. Does anyone try to discourage them from wasting their lives playing boshy records? No. There's big money in it, so you give them special programmes and tell them they're splendid and devote whole columns to their pitiful, piffling little goings-on. If any parent mentioned the word duty to their children, today, they'd laugh out loud. I dare say yours did.'

'Well no, as a matter—'

'Thought so. Take what they call the Arts. Can you stomach those pictures they turn out? Of course you can't. Nobody could look at 'em without feeling sick. D'you go to all those plays? Certainly not. Never met anybody who does. And they tell you nobody reads any more, and can you wonder?'

'Well, I do—'

'Just as I thought. I don't mind telling you that I don't understand what's going on in the world. You might say I'm a back number. Back number! Those back numbers, when you come to think of it, didn't give you four pages of reading matter to fourteen pages of damned irritating advertisement. D'you ever stop to look at them?'

'They're supposed to impress themselves on

223

your mind without your realizing it.'

'Well, let anybody try brain-washing me; they'll be sorry. Take music. If you put two four-year-olds down at a piano and let 'em bang away, you'd hear exactly what they dish out at concerts nowadays, and you wouldn't have to pay to get in. D'you get any pleasure out of it?'

'I must—'

'Knew you'd agree with me. Treat to talk to a sensible woman like you, who's kept her ideas straight. Most people you meet tie themselves into knots telling you about analytical cubism and orchestral texture. Keep up or fall out, that's the idea. Well, I've fallen out.'

They had reached the centre of the town, and Mrs. Channing paused, her eyes on the group that awaited her: the Colonel and his wife, James and Christine and—wheeling the baby round the Palace courtyard, while the two older children played nearby—the children's nurse.

'Won't you come and meet Colonel Bell-Burton?' she asked. 'He knows more about the Baronesa than I do.'

'That his wife?'

'Yes.'

'Can't say I like the look of her. I'm no good with babies, either. I think I'll take a walk. Thank you for a pleasant morning's meeting. If what you say about the Baronesa's right, I dare say I'd be wise to tell her we're leaving at once, and pay—if I've got to pay—for what we've had.'

Mrs. Channing hesitated.

'Did you ...' She paused.

'Did I what?' demanded the earl.

'Did you or James by any chance give her any idea of how long you'd be staying in Portugal?'

'How long? We weren't making a long stay. We hadn't put a day and a time to leaving, but of course when that truck hit James's car we had to ask how long that was going to hold us up. We were told it would be a matter of a couple of weeks; if they found anything serious, perhaps more.'

'If you told the Baronesa that,' said Mrs. Channing, 'your bill will be made out for a month's stay.'

The earl stared incredulously at her.

'Impossible,' he said firmly. 'Quite impossible.'

'My husband mentioned to her once—quite casually—that we might stay in Portugal for a month. We got a bill for a month's stay. We would have had to pay it but for two fortunate facts: the Baronesa had heard that you and James had arrived, and she heard that James's car was disabled. In order to get you and James in, she had to get us out—and so, you see, you saved us. But I think you ought to prepare yourself for a bill that covers at least three weeks.'

'My God!' said the earl, in slow and astounded tones.

He stood quite still, and Mrs. Channing saw a dark tide of passion colour his cheeks. His eyes, fixed on hers unseeingly, looked like little granite pebbles, and for a brief, uncomfortable moment she thought she could hear eerie, distant, ghostly but nevertheless wild and savage war cries.

Then the earl's cheeks had resumed their normal hue. Without another word, he raised his trilby aloft, replaced it on his head and marched away. Mrs. Channing walked slowly over and joined the others.

'We were just going,' the Colonel told her. 'Waited to see if you'd care to come and have a bit of dinner with us tonight.'

Mrs. Channing, with an air of almost genuine regret, said that her husband needed his sleep, and watched the Colonel and his wife lead the homeward procession of nurse and grandchildren. James, seated behind a foaming glass of beer, ordered coffee for Mrs. Channing.

'How did you get on with the old man?' he asked her.

'He told me he enjoyed his chat with me. He also said that Christine would make a good wife. Apart from that, he didn't sound very pleased with life.'

'Modern life,' corrected James. ' "Change and decay in all around I see." '

'That was roughly the theme,' agreed Mrs. Channing.

'He gave up the last vestige of hope this morning,' explained James, 'when Katie's mother asked him who the young man was who's taking up so much of Katie's time.'

'Is Charles,' Mrs. Channing asked with interest, 'really seeing a lot of your cousin?'

'They have to put in time together,' explained James, 'because Christine and I keep shaking them off. But a man can spend a lot of time in Katie's company without losing his head; he needs it to store all the facts she pours into it.'

'Where are they now?'

'Charles decided to hire a car. He and Katie got tired of sitting at the back of mine and going wherever Christine and I wanted to go—Here they come.'

Mrs. Channing, watching the two as they got out of a little grey two-seater and walked towards the café, thought they looked cool enough; they also, she noted, looked very much at ease with one another.

'Coffee or beer?' James asked as they came up.

'Neither; we're not staying,' Katherine said. 'Charles is coming to lunch with mother and me.'

'I don't want to,' Charles told them frankly. 'I keep telling Katie that after lunching with girls' mothers, I detect a subtle difference in the heretofore pleasant relations. You'll notice that since knowing Katie,' he pointed out, 'my words have grown longer and longer. I never met anybody like her. We've been sitting in a shady little pine wood and what d'you think she's been talking about?'

'When I last had time to talk to her,' James said, 'she was full of the possibility that Abraham's migration might have been purely a protest against the polytheism being cultivated in Babylonia by the Hammurapi dynasty.'

'This morning,' said Charles, 'it was fungus and fungoid pests. No personal application, of course. Were any of you aware that black rush of wheat, due to *puccinia graminis*, brought the 1916 Canadian wheat crop down by one hundred million bushels?'

'You're all most, most amusing,' said Mrs. Channing, 'but may I ask if you're ever going to give these vital minds of yours to a little sight-seeing? Sitting in pine woods is pleasant, but isn't it time you went to look at something interesting?'

'Such as what?' Christine asked.

'That Palace in front of you, for one thing. You've got time to go round it now. Why don't you?'

'Tomorrow,' said James. 'What else do you recommend?'

'Aren't you going to look at those lovely Monserrate gardens? Or the palace at Mafra?'

'Not Mafra,' Charles said firmly. 'I went there once. Those corridors are three miles long. I can only suppose that the architect thought the young princes and princesses were going to bowl hoops or ride bicycles. From the point of view of the poor tourists' feet, it's murder.'

'I,' said Mrs. Channing, 'am going over the Palace, and since there's no sign of my husband, James and Charles can escort me.'

They walked meekly in her wake, and the two girls watched them ascending the steps and halting on the topmost while Mrs. Channing tossed a coin to determine which of the escorts should pay the entrance fee.

'I'm not in the mood for palaces, but what I'd like to do,' Christine said, 'is to go to that fair they have in that other part of Sintra—what's it called?'

'São Pedro. It's held every second and fourth Sunday.'

'I know—and tomorrow's the fourth Sunday and I adore fairs.'

'It isn't really a fair. It's a large open-air market. I should like to go too.'

They sat for a time in silence. A group of little schoolboys in white pinafores passed them on their way home to lunch. A bus drove up to the Palace and its Dutch passengers disembarked. Down the steps of the Palace streamed a party of Spaniards; having paused to take photographs, they boarded a large red coach and were borne away. Two women carrying baskets of fish on their heads passed the café, talking to one another in loud, harsh voices. A pleasant feeling of abroad-ness stole over Christine: Hampshire seemed at this moment ten thousand miles away.

Her eyes came to rest on Katherine.

'Do you like Charles,' she asked idly.

Katherine seemed to consider the question.

'I find him interesting,' she said at last. 'He used to be in love with you and now he thinks he's in love with me. It must be extraordinary to have a heart you can keep giving away.'

'Haven't you ever given yours away?'

'Fallen in love? I'm not really qualified to talk about falling in love; I don't understand quite how it comes about. I noticed that most of my friends, when they were between seventeen and twenty-two, had more emotion than they could deal with. Religion seemed to afford one form of outlet, love another; they seemed to choose either prayer or passion.'

'And you?'

'I studied. The more I learned, the happier I felt. I wanted to marry, in time, but it's fairly obvious, isn't it, that there's more opportunity to study before marriage than after. I didn't feel there was any hurry to marry.'

There wouldn't be, Christine reflected soberly, for a girl as rich as this one. Men were only men, and the most decent, the most honest man must find it very hard indeed to rub the gold dust out of his eyes and see her as she was. And as she was was nice enough. Her eyes were beautiful, once you got used to the rather blank stare that looked through rather than at you. Her skin was good, though more make-up would have improved her. She had a nice figure and long, lovely legs and would, with more dress sense, be one of those lean, elegant women who wore well. She was attractive, but perhaps not quite attractive enough, without the added attraction of her wealth, to keep a swarm of men round her, ready if not eager to be picked up when she could take her mind off her studies.

'Were you,' Christine heard her ask, 'in love before you met James?'

'Not in love—but I was always, in a way, on the look-out,' she confessed. 'That jeer about a woman looking at every man she meets as a possible husband is unjustified, but I myself, from nineteen onwards, thought a lot about providing my children with a suitable father.'

'Ah! Now you're talking about Galton.'

'I'm not talking about Galton at all. Who's Galton?'

'Charles Darwin's cousin.'

'What have either of them got to do with being the father of my children?'

'Galton established the theory of what he called eugenics. He and Darwin founded the Galton and Eugenics laboratories at—'

'If you're not careful,' Christine broke in,

231

'you're going to soar into intellectual planes too high for me to breathe in. You're awfully hard to talk to, Katie—did you know?'

'People do tell me. James used to—and Charles says I don't keep to the point.'

'You do, but you sharpen it too much. Your trouble,' diagnosed Christine, 'is that you've not the faintest idea how hollow some people's heads are. Clever people like you, with their brains stuffed full, can't understand one simple fact, which is that more than half the population shuffle along all their lives knowing practically nothing.'

'You're extremely intelligent.'

'Of course I am. I'm intelligent enough to know what I don't know, and to stretch what I do know as far as it'll go. I can think straight about most problems I meet. But intellect is something else. Take this Galton and Darwin, for example. When I go home, I'll look them up; I'm willing to learn. But what you've got to understand, if you can, is that there are millions of people like me who have to think twice before they get Darwin sorted out from Newton. One was apes and the other was apple, but *which?* I had to ask myself until I was nearly twenty. It's shameful, and regrettable, and I'm honestly sorry I wasted my schooldays showing off at games and dodging lessons. I'd rather talk about Darwin and Galton than treat you to girlish confidences about the father of my children, but you've got to begin right at the bottom. Do you see?'

'I suppose,' Katherine spoke in the detached tone of one adding yet one more fact to the well-docketed accumulation, 'I suppose I'm rather a bore to talk to.'

'You're not a bore at all. I'm the bore, and Charles, and James, because our conversation is nothing but small change rattling. Once or twice, in the last day or two, I've felt that instead of marrying James, I ought to put the whole thing off and try to fill up some of the holes in my head. I came out here full of bounce, and it's been gradually seeping out of me. I can't say one word to any of these Portuguese, I can't even assemble two sentences of Spanish, my French is pathetic and I don't even know who Galton was. If I don't get back to London soon and lose myself among my fellow morons, I shall lose my self-esteem, which used to be enough for two.'

'James fell in love with you and not with me. Doesn't that prove something? If you take the biological aspect of selection, you'll find that—'

'I didn't mean you to come down to *that* level. All the same, on *that* plane I can follow you all the way. I've got two sisters who were, for years before they married, outstanding examples of the types that suggest to men, at first sight, the principles of natural selection. Want to hear?'

Katherine was still listening when the others

returned from their tour of the Palace.

'Thank you,' Mrs. Channing said to her escorts. 'I enjoyed that, but I'm afraid you didn't.'

'I did,' Charles said. 'I'm all for learning. I've been learning all the morning, and enjoying it. Did you know that humming-birds don't hum? Their sternum or breastbone is keeled to form a base of attachment for the muscles needed to vibrate their wings. And there's another thing: grafting is the union of the cambium layer or the scion or graft with that of the stock. I think. What else, Katie?'

'Idiocy,' said Katherine, 'can sometimes be traced to neuropathic stock. I must meet your parents. And now will you come and meet one of mine? The other died when I was four and—my mother told me—went to heaven.'

'The conception of transmigration,' James called after them as they left, 'according to—'

'Don't *you* start,' said Christine.

'Starting's easy; it's keeping it up that's the trick,' said James. 'Especially in my case; as you may or may not know, if the vibrating body is in a vacuum, no acoustic effect will proceed from it.'

'Personally, I'll take Katherine,' said Mrs. Channing, 'and anybody can have the rest of you. That's a nice girl, James, and if you take my advice, you'll think again before letting Charles walk off with her.'

'Your duty,' Christine reminded her, 'is to

get me off, not put him off.'

'Katie's nice enough,' James conceded, 'but Charles is right when he says she's swotted up on the wrong subjects. Show her a field of barley and she calls it wheat. Lead her up to a promising young bull and she shies away and says she doesn't like cows. And for a girl who's watched as many Test matches as she's done, she might just as well have been teaching the canary how to sing.' He rose and bent to kiss Mrs. Channing. 'Anyway,' he ended, 'Katie isn't the only nice girl. You too.'

CHAPTER TEN

On the following day, James and Christine offered the two empty seats in the car to Mr. and Mrs. Channing, and they set out on an expedition together. Once, however, was enough for Mr. Channing; he could stand, he said, being driven by James; he could even stand being driven by a Portuguese—but when James was driving in one direction and a Portuguese was bearing down on them from another, it was more than his nerves could bear. He elected to pass the days quietly with his wife, sitting on the verandah talking to Gustavo, going for short walks and joining the Colonel at the little café.

The earl came to make one of the party on

the verandah. He came uninvited, sneered at Mr. Channing's idea of a walk and warned him of the dangers of losing his temper and drinking rot-gut; nevertheless, both Mr. Channing and his wife knew that he enjoyed sitting with them, enjoyed their company, enjoyed most of all the homely atmosphere of the Pensão Pombal. Its simplicity was more to his taste than the luxury at the Quinta de Narvão; moreover, as it was now almost certain that he was in his turn to be victimized by the Baronesa, he preferred to keep out of her way until the day of reckoning came.

She had not returned the passports. The earl, walking up to the Pensão one morning after breakfast, told Mr. and Mrs. Channing that on the previous evening, the Baronesa had informed him that they were unfortunately mislaid. He had, he said, accepted her over-elaborate excuses without comment.

'Had she lost the key of the special drawer she keeps them in?' Mrs. Channing enquired.

'That what she said to you?'

'Word for word.'

'What're you going to do?' Mr. Channing asked.

The earl said nothing for a time; he had this habit, they had learned, of appearing not to have heard a question and sitting quite still, hands clasped, head slightly bowed, eyes half-closed, nor answering until he had considered the matter. More and more, in these withdrawn moments of his, Mrs. Channing sensed something powerful, indomitable. It seemed to her strange and sad that so proud a spirit should have to bow before a scheming old woman.

'I shall pay,' he said at last. 'You were quite right; once you're caught, once you're trapped, you can't get out without paying.'

'But no bill yet?' Mrs. Channing asked.

'No. I thought it was coming last night, but one or two things got in the way. The first was that I was a little late for dinner; I'd forgotten that James wouldn't be back, and by the time I realized it, I was late in changing. She doesn't like to be kept waiting, especially for meals. The second thing was after dinner, when she did the usual round of the cabinets, showing me her loot—for loot I'm more and more certain it is. She was leaning over to take out one of those little gold-and-jade figures, and I moved aside to make way, but unfortunately I brushed against her coffee cup which she'd put on a table, and the coffee spilt on that beautiful rug and there was the devil to pay. She went down on her hands and knees, mopping and moaning and screeching to me to ring the bell and I don't know what. What with learning about the loss of the passports before dinner, and spoiling the rug after dinner, it wasn't much of an evening.'

'She'll charge you a nice sum for cleaning; you wait and see when your bill comes,' Mr.

Channing prophesied.

'And of course, the bill will come.' The earl sounded resigned. 'Nasty thought, isn't it, that she's going to get away with this sort of thing, unchecked, for God knows how many more years? You were right in another thing: her most devilish cleverness lies in her choice of guest. Some people would assault her, or damage her property, or involve themselves in futile protests to the police—but she knows what she's doing: she only pins down the type—like yourselves—whose background, whose training, whose instincts all make them, in the end, decide to pay. Decency's no match for devilry. Like you, I shall pay—and get out.'

'Where will you go?' Mrs. Channing asked.

'Home. I wish I'd never left it. The only thing that got me out of it was ... well, you know quite well what it was. It was a forlorn hope, that's all. I was a silly old fool—but I'll always regret all those millions of Katie's. Perhaps your daughter'll be able to manage on what James will eventually be able to offer her, but I shan't be there to see. I'll be dead, and not before my time.'

They sat silent, each lost in thought. Gustavo's wife brought out more coffee; Gustavo chopped wood; the chickens and turkeys and geese and ducks wandered in and out of the outhouses; the cats and dogs, worn out by their nocturnal activities, slept.

When the earl rose to go, Mr. and Mrs.

Channing walked with him to the end of the lane.

'How'll you go home if the car isn't ready?' Mr. Channing asked. 'You'll have to wait for it, won't you?'

'No. It's going to be ready tomorrow or the day after, but I'm going back by air. James can make his own way back by his own route. Well ... I'm going into Lisbon. See you soon.'

'We're all going to the São Pedro fair tomorrow; are you coming too?' Mrs. Channing asked.

'No. Time I brought this thing to a head,' the earl replied. 'I shall tell the Baronesa in the morning that we're very grateful, but we mustn't trespass on her kind hospitality any longer.'

Mr. Channing remembered the morning on which he had said almost those words to the Baronesa, and remembered her reply. He recalled the agonizing humiliation that had filled him, and out of the memory he spoke feelingly to the earl.

'I'm sorry for you; more sorry than I can say,' he said gruffly. 'I wouldn't want my worst enemy to go through it.'

'I would,' said the earl. 'And you needn't feel sorry. What you haven't grasped yet is that you're a decent chap, and in every decent chap, there's a soft core. I'm hard all the way through. Tap anywhere and you'll find granite. James takes after his mother, but there's still a good bit of me in him, as I dare say Christine'll find out in time. The Baronesa hurt your feelings, but she won't hurt mine. She made you feel a cadger, and that hurt—but she'll only make me feel a damned old fool for not having been on my guard against thieving old bitches, begging your wife's pardon. In other words, I bought it, and I'll pay for it.'

'In cash,' Mr. Channing reminded him.

'In cash, yes. After my talk with you the other day, I decided that I'd be wise to avoid at least one difficulty: that is, having to stay on until I could meet the bill. I'm going into Lisbon to fix it up, and I'll go home on the first plane on which I can get a seat.'

He left them and walked away with firm footsteps, and Mr. and Mrs. Channing turned back to the Pensão.

'I'm still sorry for him,' Mr. Channing said. 'He can say what he likes, but if he's got to pay, he'll like it even less than I did.'

Mrs. Channing said nothing; for the second time, she was hearing the faint, elusive war cries. It was either an over-wrought imagination, she decided, or too many grilled sardines.

There were more grilled sardines that evening, when the four younger members returned late, one pair to talk of Obidos and Nazaré, the other of Setubal and Arrábida. They had all dined early, and were ready to eat again; James managed to convey to Gustavo an idea of what was to be known henceforward at the Pensão as a *barrr-bee-koo*, and soon there was assembled in the courtyard the little clay grill, a basket of fresh sardines, some highly coloured sausages and a large number of Portuguese friends and relations. James and Charles superintended the cooking, and everybody—family and friends—gathered round to eat. Mr. and Mrs. Channing, giving up any hope of sleep, stayed up and watched the proceedings, Mr. Channing at one end of the verandah with Gustavo, Mrs. Channing at the other, beside her a little straw stool on which one of the younger members came from time to time to rest. When Charles, a brimming glass of wine in his hand, came to see how she was enjoying herself, she asked an idle question.

'How do you manage to spend so much time away from your aunt?'

'It's really quite simple,' he said. 'I'm always instructed to stop her from doing anything particularly silly, like inviting a lot of people to meals and forgetting they're coming, or arranging large-scale expeditions and forgetting to order the bus. I decided that all of it was awkward, but none of it actually harmful, so now I'm having a lot of fun and my aunt's having a lot of fun.'

'When are you going back to England?'

'I'm leaving on the early morning plane— about three or three-thirty, I think—on

241

Monday. I've got to be back at work on Monday morning.'

'Will you be in time?'

'If you mean will I get there at the hour I'm paid to get there, no. But I'll have time to hang up my hat and sit down at my desk just three seconds before the bosses enter the door. That's being in time.'

'Katie's mother,' ventured Mrs. Channing, 'hasn't been seeing much of Katie lately.'

'Katie's mother,' Charles said, 'has only got one idea: dogs. Not dogs in general, just Great Danes. She's been spending her time finding out who's got Great Danes and going round inspecting them to see they're getting the right treatment. So that takes care of Katie's mother. I've only met her twice, but I wouldn't like to say she was really human. I gather from James that she wanted a son; when she got a daughter, she decided that the fates were against her and decided to go in for Great Danes. I wouldn't be surprised if a lot of Katie's concentration on learning wasn't to fill a gap. I don't think life with her mother could have been too satisfying.'

'She's a nice girl,' said Mrs. Channing, feeling her way.

'Katie? Katie's a wonder. If it weren't for those millions, I'd tell her so—but you have to be careful with a girl as rich as that, for two reasons: one, you have to convince yourself you're totally uninfluenced by all that money, and two, you have to convince her you're totally uninfluenced. Anybody who says that three millions makes no difference is just talking through his hat—unless, of course, he's lying.'

There was a comfortable pause. Mrs. Channing wondered whether they would have a London wedding, and whether she could appear yet again in My Grey.

'Come and dance,' Katherine called from below.

Charles went down the steps to join her in a folk dance and presently Christine, panting, came to sit beside her mother.

'How do all those old housewives at home manage to skip round doing Morris dances?' she asked. 'I'm whacked.'

'You're out of condition. Too much driving, not enough walking.'

Christine made no reply; she merely drew her mother's attention to James and Felipe who, arms intertwined, were stepping briskly to the music of an accordion.

'If James knew what he was doing, he wouldn't be doing it,' she observed after a time.

'Dancing?'

'Dancing with Felipe. Want to know something?'

'Well?'

'It was Felipe who drove that truck into James's car.'

Mrs. Channing twisted herself round to

stare at her.

'You're joking. Or guessing.'

'I'm telling you the sober truth.'

'Felipe! You mean accidentally?'

'I mean a-purpose. James didn't get the truck number, but he remembered that the driver had a rather Chinese look and a black peaked cap, and he said if he ever saw him again, he'd bash him. Look at him now, bashing away.'

'Why didn't you tell me this before?'

'No time, for one thing. James is a full-time occupation. When James wasn't with me, Father was with you. Want to hear it all?'

'I'm waiting.'

Christine told her briefly. When she had finished, Mrs. Channing sat musing for a time.

'I felt,' she said slowly at last, 'that there was something missing.'

'Could it have happened at home?'

Mrs. Channing tried very hard to imagine a young garage hand in England disabling a car in order to rescue chance-met foreigners from a trying situation.

'It might,' she said doubtfully.

'Felipe in daylight, in his black peaked cap, driving a truck,' Christine pointed out, 'isn't quite this Felipe in check shirt and jeans and with black curly hair, leaping round showing James regional dances.'

'When will you tell James?'

'When he gets the car back looking nicely

straightened out and ready for the road. I'll tell him then, and he'll see the joke. Perhaps.'

'I don't think I'll tell your father. Not until we get home. I think we'll be going fairly soon—will you mind?'

'No. But I'm coming back, and so is James.' She hugged her knees in a sudden, happy gesture. 'This is a nice country, isn't it?'

Mrs. Channing looked at Felipe and saw him in a green truck, bearing down purposefully on James's car.

'Very nice,' she agreed.

CHAPTER ELEVEN

On the following morning, Mr. and Mrs. Channing drove with James and Christine to the large open market-place at São Pedro de Sintra. They arrived shortly after ten o'clock to find the square thronged and a babel of sound arising from the crowds wandering between the covered booths, or threading their way past piles of merchandise spread out on the ground. It seemed that they could buy anything from potatoes to pack mules.

Charles and Katherine joined them at the top of the stone steps that led down to the market from the side road in which they had parked the cars. Mr. Channing, looking round at the party, decided that it would be better if they separated and arranged a time and a place for meeting again.

'There's no need to lose your heads and buy a lot of rubbish,' he warned his wife and daughter. 'You'll only end up with a lot of stuff you don't want, and as these people can see you're tourists, they'll probably charge you through the nose. Look at things, but don't buy.'

'It all looks so cheap,' Christine said.

'Nothing you don't want is cheap,' said her father. 'I shall walk round and meet you here in half an hour.'

'An hour,' said Christine. 'I've just seen a little white donkey.'

Mrs. Channing was not interested in donkeys. She made her way through the crowd in the direction of the stalls selling coarsely woven tablemats and tablecloths. Katherine and Charles went to look at the basket chairs and tables and bags and stools spread outside a little tent, and James and Christine walked to the end of the square, where cows, donkeys, goats and pigs were being sold. Wandering back, they stopped to look at the antique stalls, stood fascinated before a line of large framed photographs of Edwardian beauties, bargained for and bought a small copper jug and then met a laden, flushed and happy Mrs. Channing. She was carrying an immense straw basket filled with tablemats, little embroidered aprons, gay woollen Portuguese figures and

246

small stuffed donkeys surmounted by brightly-coloured regional figures.

'Presents,' she explained to Christine. 'There are some lovely little beaten silver fingerbowls on that stall over there, but your father unfortunately came up just as I was bargaining for them, and wouldn't let me buy them.'

'What in the world do you want fingerbowls for?'

'His very words. James, do you see those sheepskins that man is selling? He's asking three pounds, but I think I could get him down to two.'

'What on earth,' began Christine, 'do you—'

'—want a sheepskin for? For your father. He's always longed for a sheepskin-lined jacket for working in the garden on cold winter days, but I've never dared to buy him one; they cost such a lot at home that I knew he'd never be able to feel warm in one. But if I bought one of these sheepskins . . . if only I could hide it until we got home . . .'

'We'll make my grandfather take it home,' James said.

'On a plane?' Mrs. Channing shook her head hopelessly.

'We'll buy one and leave it with Gustavo,' said Christine. 'I saw him sitting outside one of those little cafés near the cars. He'd hide it if we asked him to.'

'Then let's buy one,' said Mrs. Channing. 'Come and help me, but make sure your

247

father's not around.'

There was no sign of Mr. Channing, but they came upon Charles and Katherine wandering fascinated among a pile of old rusting bedsteads.

'Take a look,' Charles invited. 'This old iron must date from the Peninsular War; only the British could sleep with those brass knobs. Where are you going?'

'To buy a sheepskin,' said Christine.

'In this weather?'

'For my father, for the winter, for the garden. Come and use those two words of Portuguese you're always showing off.'

They surrounded the sheepskin man, which might have been the reason for his dropping the price from three to two pounds. They surrounded the sheepskin in case they met Mr. Channing on their way to the road, and then they surrounded Gustavo and made him understand that he was to keep the purchase hidden away until it was asked for.

'And these too.' Mrs. Channing handed him her large, laden basket.

'Why hide those?' Christine asked in surprise.

'I'm not hiding them. I'm just keeping them out of your father's sight for a little while. It's just—'

A cry from Christine brought her to an abrupt stop. James had seized her arm and was dragging her forward, talking excitedly.

'Look, Christine, *look*! Over there. Over there near all that saddlery. There he is!'

'*Who* is?'

'The fellow who rammed my car.' James bounded away and threw a last sentence over his shoulder. 'Wait and see what I do to him.'

'James! James, come back!' shouted Christine.

They all hurried across the road, to see him leaping over the preliminary fences—baskets of potatoes, beans, peas, peppers, oranges, cherries, onions and massive pumpkins.

'James!' Christine's call floated across the square and was lost.

'Why call him back?' asked Charles, scandalized. 'If it's really the fellow who deliberately damaged his car, why yell at him to come back?'

Christine did not hear. She was watching James, who had bounded round the plastic toys and reappeared beyond the copper kettles. Now she could see where he was going—and in the centre of a group standing near the tethered animals, she at last saw Felipe.

It was, she realized, no use standing here and hoping that nothing would happen. James's face, when last she saw it, had had a look so like his grandfather's that she knew he would not, even if she could reach him, be in a mood for reasonable argument. Without wasting any more time, she turned and ran across the road to the café at which they had left Gustavo. She seized him, dragged him to the top of the steps, and pointed.

'Felipe!' she panted. 'Felipe ... Oh, can't *anybody* speak this beastly language?'

Gustavo looked round, saw no sign of Felipe, and waited for enlightenment. It came, to everybody's surprise, from Charles. Taking Gustavo by the arm, he pointed to a truck some distance away, brought his hand down violently on a car parked beside them, and in a loud, angry voice explained the situation.

'Felipe bang-bang automobile Senhor at the *garagem.*'

Gustavo's eyes swept the square. He saw Felipe, protesting vigorously, being hauled by James from among his friends. The latter, clearly determined not to give him up until further explanation was forthcoming, hauled him back again. There were several friends, and they were all strong-looking men, but James was already scattering them to right and left.

With one bound, Gustavo, less lithe than James but with a weight and force that left no doubt of his physical capabilities, was down the steps and weaving his way past obstacles. He reached the scene of action just as James, having tossed aside the protective screen and reached his prey, was squaring for an assault. Gustavo came up from behind, threw iron arms round him, pinioned him and threw over his head a rapid stream of orders. Felipe turned and went swiftly to the end of the square and was lost. Christine saw James struggling, but not until Gustavo had satisfied himself that Felipe was out of reach did he release him.

James made his way back and climbed the steps glumly.

'Lost him,' he reported, as he joined the others. 'That Gustavo came up and—'

'How dare you make a scene like that?' broke in Christine fiercely.

'Scene?' He stared at her in astonishment. 'Do you realize who that was? It was the fellow—'

'It was the fellow you were eating sardines with last night, that's who it was! It was the fellow who taught you those Alentejano dances, that's who it was!'

'Dances . . . I tell you, it was the truck driver! I told you I'd know him again. I told you—'

'Well, you didn't know him again!' Christine's voice was low but furious. 'You saw him at the Pensão last night, and you didn't know him. You thought he was a sardine griller and a dance instructor, that's all! Who do you think you are, rushing across a—'

'Don't you understand what I'm telling you? That fellow deliberately drove a truck into my car. I recognized him, and what's more, he recognized me. He knew who I was.'

'He knew who you were last night, too. And I knew who he was. But you didn't know who he was.'

James was staring at her with slowly dawning comprehension.

'Felipe? No!'

'Felipe yes. One minute you're dancing with him, and the next—'

'Are you trying to tell me,' he broke in slowly, his expression one of blank disbelief, 'that you ... you ...'

'That I knew? Of course I knew! Why would I have yelled at you to come back if I hadn't known?'

'You knew all the time,' James said, his brow black, 'that this fellow smashed up my car and—'

'If he hadn't, where would you be now?' demanded Christine. 'I'll tell you where: you'd have been on your way back home. And where would we have been? We'd have been on our way home too. And Charles would have been stuck with his awful aunt and Katie would have been stuck with her ... with her mother. Aren't you ever grateful for *anything*? A man does you a favour, and what do you do? You chase him round a market square and try to hit him.'

Mrs. Channing, glancing round at the knot of interested spectators, felt it was time to indicate that it was not James who was now making a scene. On the point of checking her daughter, she changed her mind and decided to remain silent; if they wanted to have it out, this was as good a place as any.

'May I ask,' James was saying coldly, 'why you didn't tell me before that you knew who'd damaged my car?'

'I was going to tell you when the car was all right again. I wasn't going to tell you before, because you've got your grandfather's nasty temper, only worse, and I wanted to avoid what you've treated us to just now—a public brawl. You come out to a heavenly country, you get favours done for you by one of its . . . its citizens, you grill sardines with him and learn dances from him, and then you fly off the handle simply because you suddenly remember you've seen his face before somewhere. If you want to know, Felipe works at that garage your car is at. He drove the truck into it simply to oblige us, and I hope you're ashamed of yourself, that's all.'

She came to a stop, breathless with anger. James looked from her flushed, furious face to her mother's calm one.

'You heard what she said?' he asked.

'Yes, I heard,' said Mrs. Channing.

'You followed her reasoning?'

'She merely tried to point out that you owe Felipe something. Not what you were going to give him.'

'Frankly, you've both got me addled,' James said. 'Am I to understand that this Felipe gets off scot-free after deliberately ramming—'

'Ramming, bashing, mashing—what does it matter?' broke in Christine. 'He didn't know who you were. All he knew was that once your car was out of action, you'd have to stay. Once you had to stay, the Baronesa would get to know. Once she got to know, she'd be in there with her invitation to be her guest. Once she'd trapped you, we—my mother and my father and I—were free to go, free to go without paying for the month she'd billed us for. Felipe got you in and got us out. Am I going to stand by and watch you ramming or bashing him? Am I?'

'You tell me,' said James helplessly. 'My head's going round. I suppose that next time I come across this Felipe, I've got to grill sardines with him instead of—'

'Yes, you have,' said Christine. 'And if you want to change your mind and marry someone else, you're welcome. I don't want to spend the rest of my life extricating you from free fights at fairs. You needn't try to pretend that you wanted to fight Felipe; all you wanted to do was fight. You streaked across that square all set to have a good time bashing somebody.'

'I—'

'You needn't argue. I know you. You and your grandfather too. You're both still Border bandits.'

'You know,' Katherine put in thoughtfully, 'that never occurred to me before, but I believe you're right.'

'Of course I'm right. I'm going to be chained to a gorilla for the rest of my life.'

'If anybody's interested,' said James, 'I'd like to tell them what the gorilla's going to be chained to.'

'Some other time,' said Mrs. Channing. 'I'm sure you must be thirsty, James. Isn't it time we all had a nice cool drink?'

They had to wait for Mr. Channing. James brought his car to the top of the steps, but it was some time before Mr. Channing appeared. When at last he joined them, he came with empty hands.

'Didn't you buy anything?' he asked the others.

'I looked at several things,' said Mrs. Channing. 'I'll tell you about them after lunch.'

James opened the door of the car, but Mr. Channing made no move to get in. Instead, he looked hesitatingly over his shoulder, faced his wife, grew very red, took off his hat, wiped his brow, put on his hat again and then beckoned to a very small, very dark, very laden little boy standing a few yards away.

'I just ... as a matter of fact,' he said, 'I ... well, I bought one or two things. Cheap things. Bargains, really.'

Nobody made any comment. Mr. Channing relieved the little boy of a large shopping basket, a small shopping basket, a straw handbag, two embroidered knitting bags, two striped blankets and a number of white cotton bags on which was worked the word *Pao*.

'For bread,' he explained, handing them to his wife. '*Pao* means bread. I thought ... so hygienic.'

'They'll make nice presents,' said Mrs. Channing.

'That's what I thought. Only a matter of a shilling each,' said Mr. Channing. 'Couldn't make them for three times that price.'

Mrs. Channing was about to congratulate him on his purchases when he turned once more to the little boy. Tied round his shoulders was a stout piece of string. Untying this, Mr. Channing turned the bearer round and revealed hanging behind him a sheepskin.

'I've always'—Mr. Channing's eyes, one defiant and the other full of appeal, rested on his wife—'as you know, I've always rather wanted a sheepskin-lined...'

'What a good idea to buy the lining here,' said Mrs. Channing. 'We can have it made up at home.'

'That's what I thought. Dirt cheap. That fellow'—Mr. Channing, the worst over, began to breathe more freely and to regain his confidence—'asked four pounds, which was absurd. I stuck it out and got it down in the end. If you let these chaps see you're not going to be fleeced, I mean to say rooked, they soon decide to give you fair terms.'

'I'm sure they do,' said Mrs. Channing gently. 'What did you pay in the end?'

'Just over three. Amazing value, when you

come to think of it.'

'Amazing,' said James, putting the purchases into the car.

'Absolutely amazing,' said Charles, helping him.

Mr. Channing tipped the little boy and squared his shoulders.

'Not a bad morning's work,' he said. 'I'd be glad of a drink.'

They drove in two cars to the Pensão and sat on the verandah until it was discovered that it was too late for Katherine and James and Charles to go home for lunch. Extra places were laid for them, but before going in to the meal, Christine informed James that Felipe was in the kitchen. James made his way there, and soon Mr. Channing wondered what could be the reason for the peals of laughter to be heard, but nobody felt it wise to enlighten him.

In the afternoon the four younger members drove away and Mr. and Mrs. Channing were left to doze on the verandah. Rousing, they ordered tea, drank it and strolled through the pine woods for a little mild exercise.

When they returned, it was to find a taxi in the courtyard and the earl awaiting them on the verandah. Studying his face as they went up the steps to join him, Mrs. Channing had no need to ask questions.

'She's given you your bill,' she said.

'Yes.' The earl drew it out of his pocket and laid it on a table before them. 'Take a look.'

257

They looked, and Mrs. Channing sat down slowly, her knees shaking. The sum was so large, the demand so shameless that it could only be regarded as a measure of the contempt the Baronesa felt for her victims. Sick with sympathy, she recalled the morning on which she had walked out into the garden of the Quinta de Narvão and had seen her husband's face and heard him tell the story of his interview with the Baronesa.

One day, she thought, they would perhaps be able to laugh at this. It would be a story to tell to their friends, to amuse them. But here, and today, there was nothing to smile at. This was cheating of a peculiarly mean and humiliating kind. The earl, as he had told them, was of tougher fibre than most, but his face, grim to a degree that almost frightened her, told how deep the humiliation had gone.

'Did you pay?' Mr. Channing asked at last.

'On the spot. I told her we were leaving and thanked her for her hospitality, as I told you I was going to do. Then she handed me the bill. I looked at it and told her it was no surprise.'

'But ... the rug! Good God, she could buy a new one for what she's put down for cleaning!' said Mr. Channing.

'She probably will,' said the earl. 'I asked for our passports and I told her that I was going upstairs to see my things, and my grandson's things, packed under my personal supervision. She didn't like that much. I went on to say that when I came down again, I would pay the bill in cash—but only when our luggage had been placed in a taxi and the passports were in my possession. The interview was short, but it was not sweet. I drove to the Quinta dos Castanheiros, told them the story and asked them to put me up for a night, and to keep James until he leaves Portugal. I came to say good-bye and to tell you I hope you'll come up and stay when you get back. You may as well see what Christine's letting herself in for. And now I must go.'

He refused firmly to sit down, to have a drink or to wait until the others returned.

'James'll bring Christine along to say good-bye to me this evening,' he said. 'And now...'

They shook hands and the earl took up the hat he had laid on the table.

'There's only one other thing,' he said. 'This.'

He put a hand into his pocket, drew out a small object and held it out. Mr. and Mrs. Channing looked at it, looked again—and Mrs. Channing, feeling her knees giving way again, sank slowly on to a chair. The earl replaced the little figure in his pocket and spoke briskly.

'Solid gold,' he said. 'Worth, I should judge, a good many of the bills I've just paid. Rug and all.'

Mr. Channing tried to speak, failed, cleared his throat and then brought out a husky question.

'When ...?'

'After speaking to your wife, I decided that I ought to take precautions. Once I brought myself to believe that I could be made a victim—and it was hard, I can tell you—I knew I had to do something. When she failed to produce our passports for the proposed trip to Spain, I decided I'd go for one of her trophies—but I didn't see how I could get hold of one without being seen. While I was brooding over it during dinner last night, I made a rough plan—but there was no need for plans. After dinner, she led me to a cabinet and opened it and was showing me these figures and it was then that the coffee cup fell on to the rug. Down she went on her knees, and there was my chance. I acted so quickly that I couldn't believe I'd done it. But for just that one split second, she'd been off her guard. She loved that rug as much as she loves everything else she's collected. By the time I'd rung the bell for the servants, she'd remembered the cabinet and got up and locked it, but she didn't think of counting heads. Nor will she until she opens it again for the next lot of fish she nets. But that might be before James leaves the country, and if so, I'd like you to keep an eye on him. I'm not telling him what I've done—not until he gets home. If she discovers the loss, and tackles him, she'll have wit enough to see that he knows nothing about it. But if she goes so far as to accuse me, he might forget himself. He looks mild enough, but if he's roused, he can be dangerous. That's why—that's one reason I wanted you to know. The other reason was to stop you from being too sorry for me. It doesn't make up, of course, for being made a fool of—but it's nice to know I shan't be out of pocket.'

'But if you take it—' began Mr. Channing.

'—out of the country, you were going to say. I shan't. When I went in to fix my air tickets—I'm leaving, incidentally, on the plane that leaves at dawn tomorrow—I went to see a firm of British lawyers in Lisbon, and talked to them. I'm leaving it in safe custody, to be kept until I send them written instructions to hand it over to the Baronesa. And they won't get written instructions, of course, until I've got back what I paid her, minus a reasonable charge for the time we spent with her. And plus, of course, the lawyers' fees. And now good-bye. Peculiar circumstances to have met in, but it's been a great pleasure.'

'I wish,' Mr. Channing said wistfully, 'I had half your spunk.'

The earl got into the taxi and raised a hand in farewell. 'I come,' he reminded them, 'of a race of robbers.'

CHAPTER TWELVE

Christine dined that night with James and his grandfather. After dinner, the earl retired to have a short sleep, before catching his plane, and James drove Christine to the Pensão Pombal. With Mr. and Mrs. Channing were Charles and Katherine; Charles had come to say good-bye.

They all sat on the verandah, but little was said; the holiday was, in a sense, over; the party was breaking up.

'Pity I didn't know earlier that your grandfather was going back on his own,' Charles said to James out of a long, brooding silence. 'I'd have asked you to drive me back.'

'No go,' said James. 'I'm taking Christine.'

'Couldn't Katie and I have made a foursome?'

'No. Four's too many. Besides, what about Katie's mother?'

'My mother's staying out here,' Katherine said.

'Well, four would have been too many, anyhow,' said James. 'Besides, I don't want to hurry back; I'm taking Christine by way of Roncesvalles.'

'That ought to be interesting,' said Mrs. Channing. 'I've never seen Roncesvalles. When do we start?'

James turned himself in his chair in order to get a clearer look at her.

'You don't mean to say you object?' he asked. 'Not seriously?'

'No. Only strenuously,' said Mrs. Channing.

'But if you're going to entrust your daughter to me for the rest of her life, what's against my taking her home on a leisurely cross-country drive?'

'Me,' said Mrs. Channing.

'But if Christine decided to go,' James pointed out, 'you couldn't stop her. She's over twenty-one.'

'Only a year over,' said Mrs. Channing.

James ran a hand helplessly over his head.

'It's ... it's ludicrous,' he said. 'I can reel off the names of two dozen couples who—'

'Don't bother,' Christine said. 'In a way, I agree with her.'

'Thank you,' said her mother.

'Don't think I wouldn't love to have you.' James took her hand and spoke persuasively. 'Christine and I would both enjoy having you, but it would, don't you agree, rather change the nature of the trip?'

'That was the idea,' said Mrs. Channing.

James, with a sigh, relinquished her hand and the project. 'What are your plans?' he asked Katherine. 'Staying or going?'

'Going. When Charles goes, who'll there be to talk to?' she asked with more frankness than tact. 'I'll go home. I'll go up and stay with your grandfather.'

'What—all that way up in Northumberland?' Charles asked in dismay. 'Haven't you any relations in London?'

'I've got a sort of aunt.'

'Then send her a telegram and say you're on your way. If you made an effort, you might be able to get a last-minute seat on the plane.'

'That's not a bad idea,' said James. 'Why don't you go and pack on the off-chance, Katie?'

'I did pack,' she said.

Before anybody could think of anything to say to this, the Colonel drove into the courtyard.

'Hello there,' he called, and came up the steps to join them. 'Came along to see what's going on. I understand the earl's left the Quinta de Narvão.'

'How do you know?' Mrs. Channing asked.

'It's all over Sintra,' the Colonel said. 'Even if it weren't, the sight of the Baronesa down at the docks would give the show away. Did she sting the earl?'

'Yes. But I dare say he'll get his own back one day,' said James. 'He'll give all the people he doesn't like letters of introduction to the Baronesa.'

'Well, I hope his going won't mean a general departure,' the Colonel said.

'I'm afraid it will,' Mr. Channing said. 'We're grateful to you for having found us this

264

place. Been a great success.'

'Well, it was lucky they could have you. They'll be sorry when you go—that is, all but Maria de Fatima.'

'Why won't she be sorry?' Christine asked.

'Why? Because she can't get married until you've gone, that's why. Didn't you know she was going to marry this young fellow called Felipe?'

'Yes, but—'

'Didn't you know they were going to live here?'

'No.'

'They are. They're to have the double room, and Felipe's old widowed mother's to have the single one. Perhaps I should have told you that they'd agreed to put off the wedding until you left.'

'But good heavens,' Mrs. Channing began in dismay, 'do you mean—'

'Oh dear me, dear me, there's no hurry,' said the Colonel. 'Don't you know anything about the Portuguese by this time? Today, tomorrow, this or next week—what's the difference? Once they know what date you're leaving, they'll start planning the wedding, that's all. I suppose you'll be off too,' he said to James.

'Yes.'

'Driving back alone?'

'At Mrs. Channing's request, yes.'

'I see. Quite right,' said the Colonel. 'But if you don't fancy the journey solo, why don't

you all try to get on to the *Princesa Margarida*?
Car and all. She's a good ship; first class only,
but that won't worry all you moneyed people.
She sails on Wednesday.'

'How could we get berths so late in the day?'
Mr. Channing asked.

'The agents advertised to say there were
berths available; it's pretty certain you'd get
on.'

'It would be a good idea for us,' said Mr.
Channing, 'but I don't know about James.'

'If it's a case of driving back alone or sailing
back with Christine, you can book my
passage,' said James. 'You won't mind, will
you,' he asked Mrs. Channing, 'if I take her up
on the boat deck after dinner?'

'She'll catch her death,' said the Colonel.
'Never could make out why young couples
made for the boat deck. Cold and windy and
unsheltered.'

'That keeps Mammas off it,' explained
James. He rose. 'If Katie wants to get on that
plane, we'd better go to the airport and see
what her chances are.'

The four drove away, and the Colonel
settled down for a chat with Mr. and Mrs.
Channing. When he left, Mrs. Channing was
called to the telephone, to hear Katherine's
voice bidding her good-bye.

'I got on. May I come and see you when I get
home?'

'Of course; we'd love to see you,' Mrs.

Channing assured her. 'Bring James.'

'Must be difficult,' mused Mr. Channing, when she had reported the conversation to him, 'to be as rich as that. How do things stand between her and Charles?'

'There's nothing definite yet.'

'How can a fellow with nothing propose to a girl with all that money?'

'She'll propose. She loves him, I'm pretty sure. He'd be foolish, and so would she, to let her money separate them.'

'How d'you know she'll propose?'

'I shall see to it,' said Mrs. Channing.

*   *   *

They went into Lisbon on the following morning and found that there was room for them all, and for the car, on the *Princesa Margarida*. They returned to the Pensão and told Gustavo that they would be leaving on Wednesday evening, and tried to make him understand that they had not known they were holding up the wedding of Felipe and Maria de Fatima. Gustavo, calling in Felipe to help him, said that yes, they had waited for the wedding but no, there was no hurry; the wedding papers had all been signed, the Prior had been informed, all was fixed but the actual day. If the Channings were really going, it was unthinkable that they should leave before the wedding; Gustavo would go at once and ask

267

the Prior what could be done.

The wedding was arranged for the afternoon of Wednesday. Mrs. Channing went upstairs after dinner on Tuesday evening, followed by Maria-Jose, Maria-Helena and Maria-Innocencia, and did the packing. She found it difficult to believe that they were really going home. It would be all right, she knew, once their faces were turned towards England, once their minds had swung back to Barbara and Antoinette and Nigel and Max and the children, once her husband had begun to wonder how the flowers and vegetables had fared under Hawkins, once she herself got into the kitchen and looked through the store cupboard. But it was hard to think of leaving Portugal. She found packing a depressing business, and was glad when the heavier cases were carried downstairs and hidden away under the stairs to leave more room for the wedding guests the next day.

On the morning of the wedding, the family rose before dawn. When the Channings came downstairs to breakfast, the cakes had all been made, chickens and rabbits and ducks were cooked ready for the wedding feast. The dining-room was looking festive, the verandah tables had new covers; out on the courtyard was a long trestle table on which places were being laid. A small boy trotted in on a donkey bringing a basket in which were tight little bridal bouquets. Women came in with baskets of fruit on their heads, helped to unload them and went away again. After a stand-up lunch, the younger children appeared in frilly white dresses and set off to walk to the church. The older girls dressed, Gustavo came out looking unfamiliar in a heavy brown suit; Josefina followed him in a mauve dress with white flowers pinned to the front. Last of all came the bride in a short, full dress of white lace, with a short white veil. A fleet of taxis appeared; Mr. and Mrs. Channing, James and Christine were sent away in the first one, the Lisbon garage having arranged to take James's car down to the docks for shipment.

They arrived at the church to find everybody, as was the custom, waiting outside for the bride's arrival. Felipe, crying, stood beside James and explained in a damp aside that he was crying from sensibility; weddings were happy, but moving; one had to weep.

The bride drove up with her father; in the next taxi were Josefina and as many daughters as could squeeze in; the rest of the taxi fleet brought friends and relations. The bride and her father led the way into the church, followed by the bridegroom and his mother; the guests filed in behind. Throughout the service, everybody but the Channings wept; had it been only a moment longer, Mrs. Channing knew that she would have wept too.

They drove back in procession to the Pensão, to the tables set with food and wine. At the height of the festivities, Mr. and Mrs. Channing, Christine and James attempted to take an unobtrusive departure, but they were seen off by the entire wedding party, and their taxi was cheered halfway up the lane.

The ship was larger than they had expected, and their cabins large and comfortable. There was no wind, and every promise of calm seas. Mr. Channing went below to unpack a few things while Mrs. Channing, Christine and James stood by the rail on deck watching the ship draw slowly away from the quay.

'While we've still got weddings on our minds,' James said Mrs. Channing, 'could I ask you about Christine's and mine?'

'You could.'

'Well, she and I both feel we've hung about long enough. I meant to go up north, but we feel it would be more sensible to marry first, and then I can take Christine up with me for good. We thought we might fix a date at the end of this month, if it suited you. If you'd have me, I could stay with you in the meantime.'

'Would the thirtieth be too soon?' Christine asked.

'If you mean can I make the wedding arrangements in time, the answer's yes,' said her mother.

'Well then, that's fixed,' said James. 'If I cry all through the ceremony, remember it's out of sensibility. We—' He broke off, staring at the receding quay.

'What's the matter?' Christine asked.

'Isn't that the Baronesa? There—see her?'

'Yes,' said Mrs. Channing. 'It's the Baronesa.'

'Hasn't she made a bad mistake?' James asked. 'Somebody ought to tell her that this ship is taking her late victims away, not bringing new victims in.'

'What are those policemen doing near her?' Christine asked. 'You don't suppose'—she sounded hopeful—'she's being arrested?'

'No. She's pointing to the ship and saying something,' said James. 'She's pretty excited. You don't suppose, do you, that somebody could have got away without paying?'

Mrs. Channing said nothing. The Fates, after all, had been kind. They had been spared this last scene. She thought of the earl and his trophy, and smiled.

'Go down to the cabin and fetch your father,' she said to Christine.

'All right. What do you want him for?'

'I think,' said Mrs. Channing, 'he'd like to see the last of the Baronesa.'

271

We hope you have enjoyed this Large Print book. Other Chivers Press or Thorndike Press Large Print books are available at your library or directly from the publishers.

For more information about current and forthcoming titles, please call or write, without obligation, to:

Chivers Press Limited
Windsor Bridge Road
Bath BA2 3AX
England
Tel. (01225) 335336

OR

Thorndike Press
P.O. Box 159
Thorndike, Maine 04986
USA
Tel. (800) 223–2336

All our Large Print titles are designed for easy reading, and all our books are made to last.